Vanessa su
spla
she ex

Kendrick looked

"You still owe me

He laughed. "You ... ... what you're claiming."

"I guess then you need to get up and come on," she said, her hands falling against her thin waist.

He shook his head. "Now I'm scared." He lifted his legs out of the pool of water and stood up. As he came to his feet, Vanessa took his hand and pulled him along behind her.

She led the way down the stone path toward the beach. The sky above was blue-black, just the shimmer of moon and twinkling of stars lighting the ground in front of them. When they reached the edge of the water, she turned toward him, a wide grin across her face.

Kendrick eyed her curiously. "What are you up to?"

"We're going skinny-dipping," she said matter-of-factly.

Kendrick hesitated for a brief moment, and his eyes widened in disbelief. He cocked his head ever so slightly as he stared at her. "I don't think that's a good idea, Ms. Harrison."

She laughed. "Get your clothes off, chicken. You bet, you lost, I won and I'm collecting."

His head was waving from side to side. "We need to talk about this."

"Anything I want. Isn't that what you said?"

He laughed. "I did say that."

"Then drop 'em," she said, pointing to his shorts.

She reached for the hem of her tank top and proceeded to pull the garment up and over her head.

Books by Deborah Fletcher Mello

Harlequin Kimani Arabesque

Harlequin Kimani Romance

DEBORAH FLETCHER MELLO

has been writing since forever and can't imagine herself doing anything else. Her first romance novel, *Take Me to Heart,* earned her a 2004 Romance Slam Jam nomination for Best New Author. In 2005, she received Book of the Year and Favorite Heroine nominations for her novel *The Right Side of Love,* and in 2009 won an RT Reviewers' Choice Award for her ninth novel, *Tame A Wild Stallion.* With each new book, Deborah continues to create unique story lines and memorable characters.

For Deborah, writing is as necessary as breathing, and she firmly believes that if she could not write she would cease to exist. The ultimate thrill for her is weaving a story that leaves her audience feeling full and satisfied, as if they've just enjoyed an incredible meal. Born and raised in Connecticut, Deborah now considers home to be wherever the moment moves her.

TWELVE Days of PLEASURE

DEBORAH FLETCHER MELLO

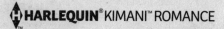

HARLEQUIN® KIMANI™ ROMANCE

To MeeMi's beautiful little angel,
Micaela Susie Mello

You are my heart and your granny loves you
more than you will ever know!

Recycling programs
for this product may
not exist in your area.

ISBN-13: 978-0-373-86377-8

Twelve Days of Pleasure

Printed in U.S.A.

Dear Reader,

I love that with each new book I am challenged to do better than the last story. It's why I *adore* the Boudreaux family. They stand firmly on a foundation of faith and family. Not without flaws, they are also perfection as much as the words on a page will allow. Kendrick and Vanessa gave me a run for my money. But like his siblings, Kendrick Boudreaux wasn't afraid to simply be the man he was raised to be and Vanessa loves that about him.

I continue to be humbled by your support. I appreciate you more than words can ever express. So, thank you! Thank you for all that you do to show me, my characters and our stories your love.

Until the next time, please take care of yourselves and may God's many blessings continue to be with you.

With much love,

Deborah Fletcher Mello

www.deborahmello.blogspot.com

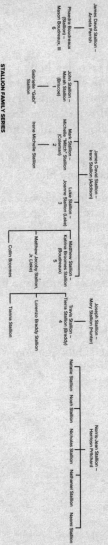

James David Stallion –
Arnela Parrish

James David Stallion –
Irene Stallion (Addison)

Joseph Stallion –
Mary Stallion (Hunter)

Phaedra Boudreaux
(Stallion) –
Mason Boudreaux III
6

John Stallion –
Marah Stallion
(Briscoe)
1

Gabrielle "Gabi"
Stallion

Mark Stallion –
Michelle "Mitch" Stallion
(Corlane)
2

Irene Michelle Stallion

Luke Stallion –
Joanne Stallion (Lake)
3

Matthew Stallion –
Katina Broomes Stallion
(Broomes)
5

Matthew Jacoby Stallion,
Jr. (Lake)

Colin Broomes

Travis Stallion –
Tierra Stallion (Brady)
4

Lorenzo Brady Stallion

Tianna Stallion

Norris-Jean Stallion –
Harrison Pritchard

Natalie Stallion   Noah Stallion   Nicholas Stallion   Nathaniel Stallion   Naomi Stallion

STALLION FAMILY SERIES

1. To Love A Stallion
2. Tame A Wild Stallion
3. Lost In A Stallion's Arms
4. Promises To A Stallion
5. Seduced By A Stallion
6. Forever A Stallion

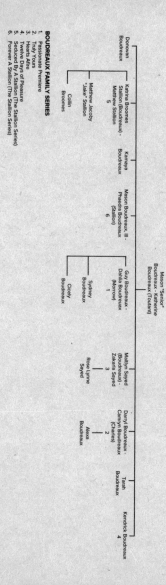

BOUDREAUX FAMILY SERIES

1. Passionate Premiere
2. Truly Yours
3. Hearts Afire
4. Twelve Days of Pleasure
5. Seduced By A Stallion (The Stallion Series)
6. Forever A Stallion (The Stallion Series)

Chapter 1

Kendrick Boudreaux took a breath, and inhaled deeply. There was a chill in the morning air and he could feel his lungs burn from the cold as they expanded. He continued to run, his long legs carrying him down the Broadway Street sidewalk. The uptown historical district was still an area of mixed residential and small commercial properties, with a wealth of 19th-century architecture, and he smiled as he reflected on his surroundings. Coming back to New Orleans always felt good and as he came to an abrupt stop in the driveway of his family home, he hoped that this time he'd be able to spend more than a week there before business sent him in another direction.

It was still dark out, no hint of morning sunshine to be found yet. Above his head, the periodic street lamp lit his way. His breathing was labored as he fought to catch his breath. He ran daily, at least ten miles, and usually the task didn't feel quite so difficult but the morning cold was unforgiving. Just days earlier he'd been running through Iten, Kenya, the temperatures in the high seventies, his heels kicking up dry dust as a bright sun shone in a deep blue sky. His tenure with the Secret Service had afforded him perks few could imagine.

He inhaled deeply, taking a series of deep gulps as he used the spare key hidden beneath a flowerpot close to the door and entered his family's home. The house was still quiet, most of his family sound asleep. It would be at least another hour before anyone else would be stirring. They had a long day ahead of them and it would be starting earlier than most would have liked. Kendrick was used to odd hours so nothing about the time disturbed him.

As he eased through the mudroom into the open family space he found his sister Maitlyn sitting at the kitchen table. She sipped on a large mug of coffee as she scanned her electronic tablet. She tossed him an easy smile as he dropped into the seat at her side.

"Good morning," Maitlyn whispered. "You're up early."

He shrugged. "Needed to get my run in before I have to put on that monkey suit."

She shook her head. "Well, I appreciate you being here to wear that monkey suit."

Kendrick smiled. "Where else would I be?"

With raised eyebrows she cut an eye in his direction.

He chuckled softly as he stood back up and moved to the refrigerator. Swinging open the door he peered inside.

"Would you like a cup of coffee?" Maitlyn asked.

"No. I'm trying to eat a clean diet. Cutting out the caffeine. You can make me a green juice smoothie if you want."

Maitlyn laughed. "I guess you missed the memo that said I'm getting married in a few hours."

Kendrick laughed with her. "Oh, I got the memo. But I know how much you like to be in control so I figured I'd give you something to do."

"Well, I don't need one more thing on my list. Make your own damn smoothie!"

Minutes later the two sat side by side, relishing their quiet moment together. Kendrick sipped his organic drink as Maitlyn helped herself to a second cup of coffee. He was in awe of his eldest sister, her calm demeanor feeling out of character for a woman who was just hours away from marrying the man of her dreams. He knew that had it been any one of his other sisters they would have been biting nails and pulling out their own hair. But Maitlyn didn't seem the least bit fazed. He couldn't help but think back to the previous year when she had met the man she would soon be marrying.

Zakaria Sayed was his best friend and the two men had been partnered together when both had been recruited for a covert division of the Secret Service. They were a consortium of global enforcement whose work was occasionally extreme, sometimes dangerous and always clandestine. Kendrick had been recruited from the FBI. His friend Zak had been with Interpol, bringing a wealth of international experience to the table. From day one they'd been fast friends and Kendrick trusted the man with his life, and now, more important, he trusted him with his sister.

Last year, Zak had become involved with Maitlyn while he'd been on a mission and she'd been on vacation. Maitlyn had gotten herself tangled smackdab in the middle of some serious mess. When she'd been abducted and left for dead, his and Zak's mission to find her had further cemented their friendship. But everything that happened had put a serious crimp in her romantic relationship, one that Kendrick had feared neither would be able to rebound from. But as his mother had often said, fate had sealed the envelope on the love those two shared.

Reunited at his family's New Year's celebration, the couple had been virtually inseparable from that moment on. Claiming semiretirement, Zak hadn't accepted any assignment since that took him away from his desk, refusing to put himself, or Maitlyn, in harm's way. Zak would soon be his brother-in-law and as the best man, Kendrick was going to ensure the two walked down the aisle without mishap.

"Hey," Kendrick said, breaking the silence. "When you get back from your honeymoon, would you do me a favor, please?"

Maitlyn met her brother's gaze. "What do you need?"

"There's a house that's listed for sale on Fontainebleu Drive. Would you check it out for me?"

"Is that the pied-à-terre with the guesthouse in the back?"

"Is it cream-colored with a wide porch and a narrow driveway along the side?"

She nodded. "I think the color's more eggshell than cream."

Kendrick gave her a daft look as a pregnant pause swept between them. He blinked, batting his thick lashes at her.

Maitlyn chuckled. "I'll check it out. Are you thinking about settling down? Maybe quitting and getting a normal job?"

Kendrick shot a quick glance over his shoulder. "As far as anyone is concerned I have a normal job, thank you very much. But I am thinking about putting down some roots. It's hard to maneuver things living in your parents' home."

"Like you live here. What's it been? Three months since the last time you were home? And if you stay forty-eight hours I'd be surprised."

He shrugged, his broad shoulders pushing toward the ceiling. "It's still hard to maneuver things."

"Which means you're giving up caffeine but not the sex and rock and roll."

"Exactly, so I need me some space to do me."

Maitlyn shook her head. "You really need to settle down."

"You're starting to sound like our mother."

"Our mother is a very wise woman."

"Yes, I am," Katherine Boudreaux responded from the doorway. She moved into the room and kissed him and then Maitlyn. "What are you two doing up already?"

Maitlyn hugged her mother back. "I couldn't sleep. I took a quick nap and then tossed and turned for an hour. Figured I'd just get up and double-check all of my lists."

"You worry too much," Katherine said. "That's why you hired a wedding planner, remember? So someone else could worry."

Maitlyn rolled her eyes. "It's not the wedding I'm worried about. I was going over everything that has to be done for Thanksgiving."

Kendrick shook his head. "That is next week, isn't it?"

Maitlyn nodded. "It's Thursday and everyone is going to be here. Mom wants to cook all of our favorite foods and the Sunday after, our brother wants to baptize the twins. Then we have to get ready for Christmas. We're all going to Texas. Everyone's staying at the Stallion ranch and there's a ton of preparing that needs to be done. I have a lot of lists!"

"And why are you up?" Katherine asked, dropping a warm palm to his shoulder.

"I had to get my run in before the day started."

"You need to get some rest, too. You both don't take nearly enough time for yourselves."

"I'm sure Zak will make sure Maitlyn gets some rest soon," Kendrick said.

His mother nodded. "And what about you?"

Kendrick grinned. "You worry more than Maitlyn does, Mom."

Katherine shook her head. Before she could respond his sisters Tarah and Katrina moved into the space, greeting them all warmly.

"Good morning, family!" Katrina Boudreaux-Stallion chirped, her toddler son sitting against her hip.

Matthew Jacoby Stallion, Jr. grinned, reaching his arms out for his grandmother. Katherine wrapped him in a warm hug, kissing his full cheeks. "How's Grandma's baby?" she cooed.

"Jake is wide-eyed," Katrina said as she handed the child over then reached for the coffeepot. "He got eight hours of sleep."

"Who gets married this time of the morning?" Tarah whined. "It's too early!"

"It's not too early," Katherine said as she leaned to give her youngest daughter a hug. "It will be a beautiful ceremony."

Tarah rolled her eyes skyward as Jake reached for her head. The baby tangled his chubby hands in her hair and pulled with all his might. He giggled, his antics tickling his spirit.

"Ouch!" Tarah exclaimed as she tried to detangle herself from her nephew's grasp.

Kendrick moved onto his feet. "I'm going to leave you women to it."

"Where are you going?" Katrina questioned as she took the first sip from her coffee mug.

"I'm headed back to the hotel. I need to get the groom to the church on time."

Tarah suddenly gave him a curious look. "What are you doing here, anyway? I thought all the men spent the night at the hotel?"

Kendrick gave her an eye roll. "They did but I had to get my morning run in."

"So you ran home?"

Maitlyn and Katrina both laughed.

"Leave your brother alone, Tarah," Katherine admonished.

Maitlyn grinned and moved onto her feet. "Do me a favor, Kendrick," she said as she walked into the other room and back, carrying a small box in her hands. "Once Zak gets his tux on would you please give him this for me?" She passed the small box into his hands.

"What is it?" Kendrick questioned as he shook the container between his palms.

"None of your business," Katherine answered for Maitlyn. "The bride asked you to give her groom a present. You get to see it after he does."

Maitlyn chuckled.

Feeling slightly foolish, Kendrick shook his head. "It was just a question," he muttered, scowling.

"Git," Katherine said, waving a dismissive hand in his direction. "We all need to get moving," she said, taking a quick glance toward the clock.

Kendrick leaned to kiss Maitlyn's cheek. The two locked gazes and Maitlyn smiled brightly at him. "You know I'm happy for you, right?" he said softly.

His sister nodded. "Make sure my guy doesn't get cold feet, okay?" she whispered back.

Kendrick smiled as he moved toward the door. "I'm on it," he said. "You know I won't rest until the job is done."

"Zak, do you take Maitlyn to be your lawful wedded wife, to love and cherish her in sickness and health, till death do you part?" the minister questioned.

"I do, sir," Zakaria Sayed said, his expression beaming with sheer joy. "I most certainly do!"

Maitlyn smiled, a tear stealing past her lashes. The beautiful couple had chosen the Oak Alley Plantation, on the banks of the Mississippi, to exchange their vows. They stood beneath the canopy of the oak tree–lined path, the first hint of the morning sun beginning to rise in the distance. The family had gathered on the lawn of the antebellum manor just after six o'clock in the morning for the intimate sunrise ceremony and Kendrick thought it had to be the most amazing thing he'd ever been witness to.

The morning air was comfortable, the last of the late-night chill keeping the rising Louisiana heat at bay. Maitlyn wore a simple knee-length sheath dress of white crochet lace over satin and three-inch heels the color of a rich cabernet. Her hair had been brushed into a loose chignon adorned with pearl combs tucked into the strands. Her bouquet was a mix of English tea roses in varying shades of orange. Her sisters, Tarah, Kamaya, and Katrina, and Zak's sister Myriam flanked her left side in simple maxi-length dresses with three-quarter-length sleeves. The floral print, in fall shades of oranges, yellows, reds and browns, was muted against an ivory background.

Kendrick and his brothers—Mason, Donovan, Darryl and Guy—stood beside Zak, the men wearing dark brown linen suits with white dress shirts opened at the neck and orange tea rose boutonnieres. As a family, they were beautiful together; as a wedding party, they were stunning.

As the family's minister pronounced them husband and wife, the first rays of the morning sun hit both their faces. Light peeked beneath the tree-lined blanket to kiss their cheeks. The small gathering of family and friends erupted in cheers. Minutes later everyone followed as the couple led the way to the veranda of the plantation home, where a morning spread of breakfast foods was laid out for the reception.

In the midst of the celebration Kendrick lifted a glass of champagne and orange juice to toast the couple. "First, on behalf of our parents, Mr. and Mrs. Mason Boudreaux, and Zak's parents, Mr. and Mrs. Hassan Sayed, we want to thank all of you for getting up before dawn to be here with us this morning. Only my big sister could manage to get people out of their warm beds so early on a Saturday morning and have y'all looking good while doing it!" He paused and smiled back at the beaming guests.

"There comes a time in everyone's life when they meet their one true love, their soul mate, the person who is going to love them for the rest of their life. That moment came for Zakaria ten years ago when he met me." Everyone laughed as Kendrick tossed his friend a wink of his eye. Maitlyn shook her head from side to side as he continued.

"Zak and I didn't become friends overnight. We had to go through some things before we learned to trust each other. It wasn't until he took me home to meet his mother and she made me her famous *m'hanncha*, a decadent orange-almond pastry, that I knew he and I would be buddies for life." Kendrick grinned as he leaned over to kiss Mrs. Sayed's cheek. "To be asked by Zak today to be his best man is an honor, but it's also honorable of him, because he's finally admitting to all of you today that I truly am the best."

Laughter rang out again. Kendrick took a deep breath, and then paused. "If someone had told me that I would be celebrating my best friend marrying my favorite sister I would have told them they were crazy. It feels like just yesterday I introduced the two as Maitlyn was headed away on a cruise by herself and I asked Zak to keep an eye on my sister for me. It gave me great joy to ask because it meant that for the first time Maitlyn wouldn't be in charge. And you all know how bossy she can be. It's one reason she's my favorite sister." He tossed the other women a quick nod. "No offense, girls."

"None taken," Katrina chimed.

"Speak for yourself," Tarah teased.

Kendrick smiled. "Anyway, it warmed my heart to ask my best friend to protect her and make sure that whoever she was spending time with made her happy and showed her a good time. It was a request I knew he would fulfill because that's the kind of man my friend Zak is. He is upstanding and honorable and a true man of his word. I really wasn't expecting him to take my request literally, so imagine my surprise when my best friend had to admit that he'd fallen in love with my sister!"

Everyone chuckled softly as Kendrick continued. "That broke all the guy codes but I had to give him a pass because my sister is such an incredible, beautiful woman that I imagine he just couldn't help himself. This union was not without some bumps along the way but thankfully I was able to come to the rescue and make things right between them. Now, it is an honor and a privilege for me to be here this morning with all of you to witness Maitlyn and Zak become one. Everything about this moment is as it should be. Mattie, I love you. Zak, welcome to the family, my friend. It warms my heart to now call you my brother." Kendrick lifted his glass and cheers rang around through the space.

By midmorning the heat was already beginning to rise. Kendrick was seated at the end of the table with his brothers Mason and Donovan.

"This was some wedding," Donovan intoned.

Mason grinned. "Maitlyn has always been able to pull off a party better than anyone else I know. Do you remember Darryl and Camryn's New Year's reception? That was over the top."

Kendrick nodded. "This has Maitlyn written all over it." He looked toward the couple. His sister was glowing and Zak was looking at his new wife with overwhelming love. "They look happy," he said as his gaze danced around the veranda. "Everyone here looks happy."

Mason laughed. "That's not a bad thing, little brother," he said as he moved back across the oversize porch.

Kendrick shrugged. His eyes skated around the space. Their not-so-little family was growing faster than he was able to keep up. Every time he went away and came back there was a new spouse, a new baby or someone who'd captured everyone's hearts while he'd been gone. He suddenly realized just how much he'd been missing out on.

He tossed an easy arm over the back of his chair as he leaned his torso back. Mason, the eldest child of the Boudreaux clan, had moved back to sit with their mother. His wife, Phaedra, stood behind him, her thin arms wrapped warmly around his neck. His brother Guy and his very pregnant wife, Dahlia, were seated at the opposite end of the table. Their father, Senior Boudreaux, was talking to Dahlia's bulging belly as if the fetus inside might talk back.

Phaedra's oldest brother, John Stallion, and his wife, Marah, were seated across from the newlyweds, all of them laughing easily together. Beside them sat John's three brothers, Matthew, Mark and the youngest sibling in the Stallion clan, Luke.

Kendrick smiled. *Matthew, Mark, Luke and John!* He could just imagine the ribbing the four of them must have gotten as kids with their biblical monikers. His sister Katrina was married to Matthew Stallion, a lawyer, and she was a district court judge. The two were constantly debating politics and legalese. They had two children, teenaged Collin and baby Jake. Kendrick could only imagine what his two nephews would aspire to as they grew up.

Kendrick smiled as Mark's wife, Michelle, waved in his direction. "You're pretty quiet sitting over there!" she chimed warmly.

"Just taking it all in, Mitch," Kendrick answered with a nod, calling her by her family nickname. "Your little munchkin is growing too fast. How old is she now?"

Mitch smiled. "Almost five," she said.

He grinned. "I like those red cowboy boots, Irene," he intoned.

The little girl just stared at him, not at all amused with his compliment. She then turned her back on him, marching off to catch up with a ball that had captured her attention.

Luke Stallion laughed, his wife, Joanne, joining in the merriment. "She's going to be a tough one," Joanne joked. "I already feel for the young boys who will start chasing after her."

"Ain't no boys going to be chasing after my baby!" Mark Stallion exclaimed. "I've already got my gun locked and loaded for any of them who even think to look in my girl's direction."

"I know that's right," Luke chimed in.

Kendrick nodded as he laughed with them. The two families were tightly entwined. And the abundance of love around the table exemplified just how deeply entangled their connection was. He took a sip of his mimosa, following it with a bite of fresh melon and forkful of scrambled eggs. His cell phone in his breast pocket suddenly vibrated for his attention.

He excused himself from the table and moved to the far end of the porch. Answering the call he listened for a moment, not bothering to say anything at all to the person on the other end. Across the room Zak met his gaze and nodded as he disconnected the call. Kendrick's gaze shifted to his sisters, who had leaned in to have their photo taken, Phaedra snapping the shot with her camera.

There was no missing the Boudreaux lineage. Their features were distinctive, each of them with slightly angular eyes, thin noses, high cheek lines and full, pouty lips. Side by side they were a kaleidoscope of colorations that ranged from burnt umber to milk chocolate.

Kendrick's brother Guy and Guy's wife, Dahlia, suddenly exited the home, both with a baby in tow. Kendrick shook his head. He had missed the births of his new niece and nephew, the twins, Cicely and Sidney Boudreaux, when he'd been away on his last mission. He suddenly imagined them walking and talking by the time he would see them next and the thought didn't sit well. He blew out a deep breath.

Zakaria had moved to his side. "You off?"

Kendrick nodded. "Yeah. A pickup and delivery. I won't be too long. It should only take a couple of hours. With any luck I'll be back in time to see you two off on your honeymoon."

"I'll hold you to that," Zak said. He took a quick glance down to the new Breitling watch on his wrist. The wedding present from Maitlyn was an 18K rose-gold design that complemented him nicely. The gesture had made both men a tad misty when Kendrick had delivered it earlier.

"So, where are you two going, anyway?" Kendrick asked.

Zak shrugged. "I don't have a clue. Your sister made all the arrangements."

Kendrick laughed. "You asked for this."

His friend laughed with him. "Yes, I did."

There was a moment's hesitation that shifted between them. "Do you miss it?" Kendrick suddenly asked.

Zak paused for a moment as he reflected on the question. "No. I thought I would. But I really don't. I would miss your sister more."

Kendrick nodded. "Kiss Maitlyn for me. Tell her I had to run an errand."

"Tell her yourself," Maitlyn said, appearing suddenly. She moved to stand beside her husband. She slid into Zak's arms, tilting her head to give him a deep kiss. When she pulled away she turned her gaze back to her brother. "Where are you running off to now?"

"Business calls. You know how it goes."

Maitlyn nodded. "Stay safe, please."

He winked an eye in her direction. "Don't I always?"

Zak chuckled softly as he slapped him on the back. "We're here if you need us, my friend."

Kendrick laughed, pointing his index finger at the man. "Friend? We're brothers now, boy! And don't you forget it!"

Chapter 2

The sound of gunshots sent Vanessa Harrison into hyperdrive; her heart raced a mile a minute. Sprinting into the family room she found her goddaughter, Gabrielle Medina, flipping channels on the home's oversize, flat-panel television. The channel was paused on an episode of *Law & Order*. Vanessa blew out the breath she'd been holding, shoulders slumping in relief.

"Gabi, why are you playing with that remote, little girl?" she said as she pulled the device from the toddler's hand.

As Gabrielle's bottom lip pushed into a deep pout, Vanessa flipped the channel back to the cartoon station. Before the child could skew her face to cry her attention was diverted to a show Vanessa didn't recognize—

some strange animation of a cow and a chicken playing on the big screen.

Vanessa moved from the family room back into the kitchen, needing to fill the baby's sippy cup with fruit juice. A federal agent followed on her heels, standing with his arms crossed in front of himself as she peered into the refrigerator. An agent had been following her from room to room for days now.

Federal agents had taken over the Medina home after Gabrielle's parents, Alexandra and Paolo, had both been gunned down. The couple had simply been in the wrong place at the wrong time. Hours after the last gunshot had echoed through the air, federal agents were holding Vanessa hostage in protective custody, because of who her father was. All she wanted to do was return home. She hadn't bargained for this drama when she'd come to visit her best friend and her family. Drama was what she'd been running from.

Weeks ago, Vanessa had been sitting in class at Columbia University's School of the Arts. With her relationship mess beginning to take its toll, the graduate film program had been the only bright spot in her day-to-day activities. A year earlier she had moved from her parents' home to New York City to be with her boyfriend, Jarrod, a law student at New York University. Things had been all good in the beginning. Then their conflicting schedules, disagreements about money and Jarrod's obsession with other women had come between them. Finding Jarrod in their bed with their red-haired neighbor had been the final straw.

It had been her best friend, Alexandra, who'd insisted

Vanessa come to Miami to spend the holidays and clear her mind. Leaving the New York cold for the Miami sun was supposed to take her mind off her problems and help her find some clarity in the chaos that had become her life. Both had figured the time away would help her heal her broken heart. After some intervention from her father the school had granted her a leave of absence, and the day before Halloween she'd landed at Miami International Airport hoping to escape everything that had been wrong. Vanessa was now wishing she'd joined her mother in Italy instead.

She sighed as she undid the cap on the bottle of Welch's white grape juice. "I really need to call my mother," she suddenly said, turning to stare at the man who was watching her too closely.

"Yes, ma'am," he said. Those were the only words he ever seemed to utter when she asked a question or made a statement.

"I need to call her now," she persisted.

A voice rang from the kitchen's entryway. "Your parents know that you're safe," a woman answered. She was tall and slim and almost matronly in the uniformed black suit she wore. "I've talked to them both personally."

Vanessa met the woman's dark gaze. "Who are you?" she asked.

"Supervisory Special Agent Kelly Layton."

Vanessa eyed the woman warily.

She dropped her gaze back to the cup in her hand as she secured the cap. "So can you please tell me what's going on?" she asked.

The other woman nodded, gesturing toward the other room. "Why don't we get the little girl settled down first," she said.

SSA Layton followed Vanessa back into the family room, where Gabrielle sat in the corner of the oversize sofa still staring at the cartoon playing on the big-screen television. Not quite two years old, little Gabi was a bundle of pure energy, and her sitting still for longer than ten minutes was a blessing. Barely turning her eyes from the animation playing out across the screen, Gabi took the cup from Vanessa's hands and lifted it to her lips. Vanessa smiled as she sat down beside the child. She then turned to stare at Agent Layton.

The woman gave her half a smile as she sat down on the opposite end of the leather sectional. "Vanessa, the man who…" She shifted her eyes toward Gabi as she paused, suddenly mindful of her words as she continued. "Marcus Bennett has been a difficult man for us to find. He's wealthy and well-connected and right now we don't have eyes on him."

Thoughts of Marcus Bennett caused her skin to go cold. She wrapped her arms around her torso to ward off the sudden chill. Just weeks earlier she and her friends had been guests on Marcus Bennett's luxury yacht. Paolo had introduced them, the two men good friends for even longer than she and Alexandra had been. Paolo and Alexandra had deemed him the perfect rebound relationship for Vanessa since she wasn't looking for forever with any man at the moment. Her friends had figured Marcus could be someone to take her mind off everything else. And he had.

Marcus had been intriguing, with a hint of street appeal and a whole lot of swag. He reminded her of the singer Akon, dark and brooding. He had an engaging smile, and physically he was built like a brick house, a hard body of solid, well-developed muscle. The man was all kinds of sexy, his appeal overshadowing his obvious illegal business dealings. He had been the perfect bad boy, the too-smooth, silver-tongued devil that mothers warned about and fathers met at the door with a shotgun. Marcus had been perfect, right up until he'd gunned down one of his adversaries and her best friends had been caught in the cross fire.

Tears misted her eyes and she swiped them away with the back of her hand. She turned to look at Gabi, who was watching her curiously. She forced a smile and winked an eye at the little girl. "Do you like that show, Gabi?" she asked, brightening her tone.

Gabrielle giggled and pulled her cup back to her mouth. The little girl was sleepy and her eyes were heavy as they shifted back toward the television.

Vanessa took a deep breath and turned her attention back to the agent. "So what happens now?"

The agent was nodding her head. "Until we have him in custody, and you can testify against him, we're going to have to keep you in protective custody."

"Testify? Why do I have to testify? I didn't actually see him do anything!" Vanessa was suddenly flustered, her eyes skating from side to side. "I can't testify! I'm not going to do that!"

"It will be okay," Agent Layton said. "You'll just need to testify about your relationship with Mr. Bennett. About what you did see when the two of you were together. Vanessa, your testimony is going to be crucial to our getting a federal indictment against this man."

"You don't understand," Vanessa started, "my diplomatic immunity…"

"Your diplomatic immunity has been waived by your father. He has given us his full support and cooperation in this matter."

"My father wouldn't do that," Vanessa said, her eyes wide.

"Your father understands the importance of getting a man like Marcus Bennett off the streets."

"Well, I want to speak with him."

"That's not possible. Once we get you out of Miami and we know you're safe then we'll make arrangements for you to speak with your family."

Vanessa shook her head. "What about Gabi?" she asked. "What's going to happen to her?"

"Arrangements are being made for her. Mr. Medina's attorney says that the father's parents are listed as her next of kin. Apparently they live somewhere in Mexico. Your father is helping us with the search to find them. Until then, we'll place her with a nice foster family who'll look out for her."

"But it's almost Christmas! Her presents are already wrapped. Alexandra's been buying and wrapping gifts for her all year. She has to have the presents her mommy bought for her!"

The agent nodded. "We'll take care of it."

Beside her Gabi had finally drifted off to sleep, completely unaware that life as she knew it was gone.

* * *

The helicopter hovered above the large Miami estate as Kendrick Boudreaux assessed the situation below. As expected there were two tactical teams in place and no signs of anything out of order. This was a simple package pickup and delivery and by the good grace of God he wouldn't even have to unholster his weapon. He liked missions like this one—an easy in and out that didn't require him putting himself or his team in too much danger. Kendrick's tenure with the Secret Service usually put him in situations that took some maneuvering to get out of. His missions with the FBI had looked like child's play in comparison. He signaled for the pilot to land.

Minutes later he took off his headphones as the pilot shut down the UH-60 Blackhawk aircraft. Exiting, Kendrick ducked low against the slowing whir and blow of the helicopter's blades. He crossed an expanse of perfectly manicured lawn, shifting into work mode as a squad leader met him at the entrance to the large home. The man led him through the foyer, into the living space. He was surprised to find Kelly Layton, one of the unit directors, standing in wait. Kendrick bristled, something suddenly not feeling right. He could count on both hands the number of times a unit director had ever shown up for a simple package pickup, and still have ten fingers left.

He nodded his head in greeting. "SSA Layton, what brings you here?"

She tossed him a quick look. "It's good to see you, too, Boudreaux," she said as she began to brief him.

"Your package is a key witness against a local kingpin named Marcus Bennett. He's wanted by this agency and a half-dozen others for crimes that run the gamut from financial fraud to human trafficking. Our witness was there when he gunned down his competition and a room full of civilians got in the way. She also has firsthand knowledge of his business dealings with Pedro Fierro, one of the victims."

Kendrick tensed. "Pedro Fierro of the Umberto Harbor cartel?"

"You know him?" Layton questioned, lifting her eyes to meet his.

He nodded. "Sayed and I took down his predecessor on one of our last assignments."

"Well, Marcus Bennett took Fierro out. Our witness was personally connected to Bennett. We also think she knows more than she's willing to say. We need her."

"So where's she going?" Kendrick asked.

"The safe house in Baton Rouge. They're expecting you."

"Baton Rouge?" Kendrick paused. He took a deep breath. "Why Baton Rouge?" he asked.

She shrugged. "Those are the orders." Layton gestured for him to follow her.

As he moved into the home's open family space, Kendrick's eyes assessed the room, shifting rapidly from one side to the other. There was an adorable little girl jumping up and down on the family room sofa, her eyes wide with curiosity. Behind the child stood an extremely attractive young woman whose own eyes were narrowed suspiciously. Concern blanketed her demeanor and Kendrick instantly sensed that she would have given anything to have been as far away from them all as she could. Layton made the introductions.

"Vanessa Harrison, this is Agent Kendrick Boudreaux. You're going to be in his custody until you get to the safe house."

Kendrick met the woman's intense stare, her gaze skewering him where he stood. Vanessa was tall, nearly as tall as him. And she was lean, with a nice hint of curve to her hips and breasts. She had a dancer's build, and he imagined her movements would be easy and graceful. She was wearing a white sundress that billowed around her body as it complemented the sun-kissed tone of her warm complexion. Her hair was jet black, the extensive length falling to the middle of her back. She bore a striking resemblance to the Puerto Rican fashion model Joan Smalls, a woman who had graced the cover of a recent *Sports Illustrated* swimsuit edition. It was the only copy of the magazine that Kendrick had ever kept.

SSA Layton suddenly stepped out of the room. Vanessa's eyes followed her for a brief moment before shifting back toward him. He smiled, the warmth of it soothing the tension between them.

"Are these all your bags?" he asked, gesturing to the leather luggage that rested on the floor in the doorway.

She nodded. "Mine and Gabi's," she answered, gesturing to the little girl, who was leaning against the sofa back as she stared at them.

Kendrick nodded.

There was still something about the situation that

didn't feel right to him. Something felt off. Why was Layton there? And why the safe house in Baton Rouge, a property that sat smack-dab in the middle of cartel ter-ritory? A house that had been compromised previously? Fierro's name attached to this meant there were bigger players involved, even if the man was dead. Where did Bennett fall in the bad-guy hierarchy? And just how much did the beautiful woman standing in front of him really know? Nothing about his orders felt right. Trust-ing his instincts, he was suddenly on edge. He stole a quick glance at the watch on his wrist.

Layton suddenly stepped back into the room. "Change of plans," the commander noted, pressing her hand to the earpiece in her ear. There was a moment of hesitation as she paused, listening to someone on the other end.

Kendrick and Vanessa cut an eye at each other, both knowing that nothing good could come from plans being changed so sudden.

"You have new orders, Agent Boudreaux. I need you to take Ms. Harrison and disappear. Are you and Sayed still in touch?"

Kendrick nodded. "Yeah," he said, not bothering to mention that the man had just married his sister. "We speak every now and again."

"Leave a number with him. No one else should know where you are or how to get in contact with you. When we can be sure about Vanessa's safety, I'll pass a mes-sage on to him. You are not to trust communications from anyone else."

Kendrick's gaze skipped from side to side. "But where…? How long…?"

Layton held up her hand. "Those are your orders. And you need to leave now. We might have a situation." She held out Vanessa's cell phone, a text message on the screen.

"That's my phone," Vanessa suddenly exclaimed. She took a step forward then stopped.

Kendrick took the appliance from Layton's hand and read the message quickly.

"What does it say?" Vanessa chimed.

Kendrick lifted his eyes to meet hers. "'I have eyes on you. You can't hide,'" Kendrick said, reading the text message out loud.

Vanessa's eyes widened. She took a deep breath.

"Agent Boudreaux will keep you safe," Agent Layton intoned.

Vanessa reached for Gabrielle, pulling the toddler into her arms. "I'm not leaving Gabi."

Layton shook her head. "That's not possible. Gabi's going to be fine."

"You don't know that," Vanessa stated. "Her parents trusted me. So until you find her grandparents and I can personally hand her over to them, I am not leaving her," she said emphatically. "Either she goes with me or I don't testify, and I don't care what my father promised you. I can go back to the embassy. It doesn't matter to me."

Chatter on all their radios interrupted the moment. Layton tossed Kendrick a questioning stare, their exchange silent. She turned and moved back into the kitchen, Kendrick following on her heels.

"Who's her father?" Kendrick questioned.

Layton was leaning against the kitchen counter, strumming her fingers against the countertop. She tossed him a look. "Alonzo Braga, the Mexican ambassador to the United States."

"She doesn't use his name?"

"He's very high profile. She said she didn't want to be associated with his politics. So she uses her mother's maiden name."

Kendrick nodded, understanding washing over him. That tiny piece of knowledge suddenly put everything in perspective. "She doesn't have to testify and legally we can't hold her."

"That's correct. She has diplomatic immunity. But that doesn't stop Bennett from wanting her dead. So her father is cooperating and he has given us his consent. The business Bennett and Fierro dealt in crossed the border into both our countries."

"What about the kid?"

Layton shrugged. "The child is just going to slow you down. But if she insists, I don't know what else to do. We need her to testify!"

He hesitated as he met the woman's anxious gaze, then he nodded. "I'll handle it," he said.

Kendrick moved back into the family room. He crossed the room quickly, lifting the toddler from Vanessa's arms as he looped an easy arm around her waist. "We have to move," he said, his eyes locking with hers. "Now!"

They were strapped into the helicopter before Vanessa could protest. Gabi squealed excitedly, her chubby fingers pointing to the house and grounds below. They spied the caravan of white-paneled trucks that careened through the home's front gates. And then just like that everything and everyone in Miami was behind them.

Vanessa looked from Kendrick to the pilot and back. Kendrick was seated on the other side of Gabi, a protective arm wrapped around the little girl. The man was breathtakingly attractive, tall and solid, with the most intoxicating eyes. His distinctive features were chiseled, his complexion a rich, warm shade of milk chocolate. Under any other circumstances she would have found his bad-boy aura intriguing.

She turned back to stare out at the landscape below, reflecting on the circumstances that had suddenly thrust them together. The weight of it must have reflected on her face, as Kendrick suddenly squeezed her shoulder. His light touch was gentle and easy. When she turned to look, the man was smiling at her. Vanessa smiled back, just a smidgen of a bend to her mouth. He suddenly said something into the microphone attached to his helmet and she realized the pilot and him were talking back and forth between themselves. Though she wasn't privy to the conversation, the only sound she heard was the loud drone of the helicopter ringing in her ears.

"Can you get me a secure line and connect me to Sayed?" Kendrick asked.

The pilot nodded, then seconds later Kendrick's earpiece clicked in his ear. There was a low hum and then a brief moment of silence.

"Problems?" Zak Sayed asked when he answered the line.

"I hate to bother you," Kendrick started as he explained the situation he was in.

"Have you had a chance to talk with the witness yet?" Zak asked when he was done.

"Not yet."

"Let me make some calls and see what I can find out but I think you're right. Something about this doesn't feel right."

"I'm glad we're still in sync with each other."

Zak chuckled softly. "You know my wife is going to kill us both, right? I'm thinking all of your sisters might have some issues with this."

"Might?" Kendrick laughed. "We're talking about the Boudreaux women, man. You've met them, haven't you? Maitlyn, Katrina, Kamaya, Tarah? Especially Kamaya and Tarah. They'd be mad at your funeral and you'd know it! I guarantee Maitlyn's going to be furious as hell!"

Zak laughed with him. "We'll worry about that when we have to. Until then, what do you plan to do?"

Kendrick shrugged. Vanessa was staring out at the land below, her brow furrowed with worry. The little girl was wide-eyed, excitement shining in her bright eyes.

"I'm going to keep her safe," Kendrick said matter-of-factly into the microphone.

An hour later Kendrick had checked them into a motel in Mobile, Alabama. Vanessa and the baby had sat in a rental car while Kendrick had leaned across the counter in the motel's office flirting shamelessly with the desk clerk. Vanessa watched him intently as he dazzled the young woman with his charm. She could only begin to imagine what he had to be saying to her. The girl giggled as he took the room key from her hand, winking an eye as if they shared some special secret.

As he stepped back into the car she tossed him a look, annoyance furrowing her forehead.

"What?" he questioned, eyeing her curiously.

Vanessa shrugged her shoulders. "Nothing."

He smiled. "Oh, it's something."

She rolled her eyes, tossing her gaze to the parking lot outside the window. "Is this where we're staying?" she questioned.

He shook his head. "No."

"Then why are we here?" she asked as she turned back to stare at him.

He didn't answer. Instead, he steered the car to the back of the building and parked. Exiting the vehicle, he unlatched Gabi from the car seat in the rear, lifting the child into his arms. She'd been sleeping since they'd picked up the car and Vanessa hoped that she was tired enough to sleep for just a little longer.

Kendrick then gestured for Vanessa to follow him.

Their room was on the second floor of the motel; the front door faced the balcony that looked over the parking lot. Inside, the space smelled like mildew—musty and dank. The rancid odor had them both frowning as they moved inside and secured the door. The room was decorated with two full-size beds, a desk and an old television set. The carpet and bathroom had both seen better days. The walls were thin and a television blared from the room next door.

As they moved inside, Vanessa shot Kendrick a look to show she was not pleased. She suddenly felt spoiled and pretentious, but if she needed to take a shower there was no way she was doing it in that bathtub. She took a deep breath, looking for the right words to voice her displeasure. Biting her tongue instead she dropped her luggage and Gabi's diaper bag onto the first bed and moved to the wooden chair in front of the desk and sat down.

Kendrick moved to lay the baby down and Vanessa suddenly jumped back to her feet.

"Wait!" she snapped. She moved to the diaper bag and pulled a blanket from inside. She laid it down across the bed top. "She might catch something if you put her on that bedspread," she said, her face twisted with distaste.

Kendrick smiled as he laid the child on the oversize, pastel-colored receiving blanket. As he stood back up, Vanessa looked satisfied. She moved back to her seat. Before either could say anything else Kendrick's cell phone chimed.

Chapter 3

Vanessa's reaction to the no-tell motel had been expected. He stood watching as she bit down against her bottom lip, her eyes taking in every strand of dust and dirt that marked the space. When something bug-like scurried across the floor her eyes widened, following it as it disappeared beneath the dresser. Her head waved slightly as she wrapped her arms around her body, hugging herself tightly. He was impressed that she hadn't gone screaming from the room. He thanked the man on the other end of the phone and ended his call. He met the look she was giving him.

"Really, we're not staying," Kendrick repeated, a slight smile pulling at his full lips.

"Then why are we here?" she asked again.

"I can't explain just yet," he said.

She nodded but said nothing.

"If you needed to let your family know you were okay, who would you call?" Kendrick asked.

"My mother."

He nodded. "Use the motel phone and call your mother. Don't tell her where you are, just let her know you're okay and that you'll give her another call soon."

"I can speak to my mother?"

He nodded, gesturing toward the motel room's phone. "Just keep it short and sweet, please," he said.

Vanessa moved to the side of the bed and reached for the receiver. Before dialing the long-distance call she grabbed a tissue from the box on the nightstand, wiped down the mouth- and earpiece and then pulled it to her head.

Kendrick chuckled ever so softly.

Joy painted her expression as she dialed, and Kendrick heard the device finally ringing on the other end. But the excitement on her face diminished quickly. Obviously, there was no answer and she must have reached her mother's voice mail instead. She took a deep breath and left a quick message. "Hi, Mama! It's me, Vanessa. I just wanted you to know that I'm okay. I'm with..." She hesitated as she tossed him a quick look. "I'm with a friend right now and I will call you back as soon as I'm able. I love you, Mama!"

As she hung up the receiver she looked as if she were struggling not to burst into tears. Sensing her distress Kendrick moved to her side. "Are you okay?" he questioned as she lifted her gaze to his.

"Do I look like I'm okay?" she hissed behind clenched teeth.

He grinned, holding his hands up as if surrendering. "Sorry," he said softly as she pushed past him, moving back to her seat.

Gabi shifted against the bed, rolling onto her side as she pulled her legs to her chest. She curled her body into a fetal position. Kendrick and Vanessa stopped to watch her, both holding their breaths that she wouldn't suddenly wake up. The little girl deeply inhaled and then snored ever so softly. Eyes wide, their gazes shifted back toward each other and held the stare. Kendrick found himself smiling and unable to contain herself, Vanessa smiled with him.

She shook her head. "This won't last too much longer," she whispered. "You better enjoy it while you can."

Kendrick nodded. "I need you to unpack some of your things. Hang something on those racks over there. Leave your toiletry bag, a pair of shoes, whatever. We'll replace them later. And most of the baby's things, too. Leave a few diapers on the bathroom counter. Maybe a bottle. It needs to look like you were here and you're planning on coming back," he said as he moved to the second bed and pulled back the covers.

He pulled a second phone from his pocket and dialed. "We should be there in the next two hours," he said into the receiver.

"I needed to make sure we didn't pick up a tail," he was saying. He paused to listen before speaking again. "I'll contact you when we get to our final destination," he responded. He took a deep breath, his gaze meeting hers as Vanessa stared at him.

He ended the call without further comment, dropping his cell phone against the pillow. "Just pack some bare necessities for the two of you in that small bag. We're going to leave the rest," he said as he moved to the bathroom and turned on the water faucet.

Minutes later he moved back into the room dressed in a pair of black denim jeans, black Timberlands and a bright white V-necked T-shirt. He then moved to the television, adjusting the volume just loud enough for others to know it was on.

Vanessa's expression was incredulous but she didn't bother to question him. When she had done as he'd asked, he scooped Gabi back into his arms and they left. Vanessa was headed in the direction of the car when Kendrick stopped her. "This way," he said. "We're taking the bus."

Vanessa hesitated, her eyes blinking rapidly as she stood staring at him. "The bus?"

Kendrick nodded. "What? Haven't you ever ridden a bus before?"

By the time they reached their final destination Vanessa was exhausted. The bus ride, with two transfers, had landed them in front of a taxi stand. A taxi ride later they were at a private hangar at the airport. The private plane was more to Vanessa's liking, and she'd even been able to catch her own nap while Kendrick entertained Gabi, who seemed to be enamored with the buckles on the seat belts.

"Where are we?" Vanessa asked when they finally landed, a team of technicians pushing the plane into another private hangar.

"Everything's going to be fine," Kendrick said.

She clutched Gabi a little tighter to her chest. "That's not what I asked you," she snapped.

Kendrick met her stare.

"Eat, eat!" Gabi suddenly exclaimed as she pulled a thumb into her mouth. "Eat, eat!'

Vanessa shook her head. "What was I thinking? She is so off schedule. It's well past her lunchtime and I don't have anything else left in this bag. She's hungry and I need to get her something to eat."

Kendrick smiled again and Vanessa, despite her reservations, found herself instantly comforted by the gesture. He tickled a finger beneath the folds of Gabi's chin. "We need to get you something to eat, baby girl!"

He pulled a cell phone to his ear, depressing the speed dial. Vanessa could tell by the change in his tone that he was talking to a woman. The thought suddenly irritated her. How dare he call some other woman when he was supposed to be focused on her? She felt herself stiffen with resentment. He caught her staring and tossed her another smile, oblivious to her sudden stress. Then he turned and walked toward the other side of the room, moving himself out of earshot. "Really, I need to get her something to eat," she persisted when he finally moved back to her side.

"I know," he said. "And probably a diaper or two, as well. It's being handled. But right now we really need to go."

Annoyed, Vanessa heaved a heavy sigh. "You still haven't told me where we are."

"New Orleans," Kendrick said.

"We're hiding in New Orleans? Really?" Her tone was just sarcastic enough to imply that he didn't have a clue what he was doing.

Kendrick laughed.

"No, we're just making a pit stop. We need to pick up some supplies."

Vanessa's gaze narrowed. "I thought you were taking me to some safe house. Why do we need to pick up supplies? I'd think the house would already have them."

Kendrick continued talking as if he hadn't heard her question. "If anyone asks, you and I are old friends. They don't need to know any of your personal business and do not, under any circumstances, tell them anything about what happened in Miami or that I am with the Secret Service."

"Who's them? Who are you talking about?"

"My sisters," he said as he guided her to a luxury BMW.

Confusion washed over Vanessa's expression. "Hold up. I thought we were going to some safe house."

Kendrick cut an eye at her. "Trust me. You'll be much safer where we're going than you'll be anywhere else for the moment." He plucked Gabi from her arms and secured the baby into a car seat, then gestured for Vanessa to get into the car.

"Look, Agent," Vanessa started.

"Kendrick. Just call me Kendrick. Please," he said, cutting her off midsentence.

Vanessa opened her mouth with a snappy retort but Gabi interrupted them both. The little girl started to cry, a loud boo-hoo-hoo that vibrated throughout the car. "Want eat!" she screamed as she kicked her legs in frustration.

Kendrick laughed. "That one has a set of lungs on her! Baby girl better catch a clue before she's riding on the roof!" he teased.

Vanessa didn't find anything funny. "She's a baby. Her entire world has just blown up and now we can't even find her something to eat. This is ridiculous!" she cried, her own tears finally falling over her cheeks.

Her frustrations had finally boiled over. Vanessa sobbed as he maneuvered his way through the streets of downtown New Orleans.

Kendrick took a deep breath and then another. As he pulled into the driveway of his family home his friend Zak was standing in the driveway.

Zak moved to the driver's-side window and the two men exchanged a quick look. "I'll go get Maitlyn," Zak said when he saw the woman and baby crying hysterically in the backseat.

Kendrick turned around in his seat. He passed Vanessa a tissue from the box in his center console. "I'm sorry," he said softly. "I didn't mean to make light of your situation. Trust me when I tell you I do understand. Your life right now is in turmoil and you're not sure if it's ever going to be okay again. But I promise you, if it takes everything I have to make things right for you, I will."

Vanessa stared at him. She swiped at her eyes with the back of her hand, her head nodding slightly. Kendrick exited out of the driver's side and opened the back door. He reached to unleash Gabi from her seat, cooing gently to ease the little girl's cries. Gabi's screams softened to a low hiccup. Her chubby cheeks damp with tears, the little girl laid her head on Kendrick's chest, snuggling easily against him as she pulled a thumb into her mouth.

Kendrick introduced them. "Vanessa, this is my sister Maitlyn. And this is Zak. They just got married this morning. Maitlyn, this is Vanessa. She's the woman I called you about. And the little munchkin here is Gabrielle. They're hanging out with me for a few days."

Maitlyn smiled. "Come on in. No one else is back from the reception yet so you're good for at least another hour."

Kendrick laughed. "We'll take an hour. That'll give us all some time to get our story straight."

Maitlyn moved to where Vanessa stood staring at them. "It's nice to meet you, Vanessa. You look like you could use some food and rest, too," Maitlyn said as she extended her hand in greeting.

Vanessa nodded. "Thank you. I need to feed the baby first."

"Don't worry. There's plenty of food inside and we stopped by the market and picked up diapers, bottles and a few things we thought you might need."

Moving into the house ahead of them Gabrielle was giggling, a cookie gripped tightly in each hand as Kendrick made faces at her.

* * *

Maitlyn and Vanessa were chatting comfortably as Gabi raced around the backyard, screaming excitedly as she played with a large ball. Kendrick stood watching them all from the kitchen window when Zak moved to his side.

"You were right," the man said, his arms crossed over his chest.

"I usually am," Kendrick replied.

"There's a car outside that Alabama motel with four very unsavory-looking guys inside. They seem to be waiting for instructions."

Kendrick nodded. "I've bought us a few hours of time but not many."

"Why'd you bring her here?"

"Because no one will connect her to me. It doesn't make sense. Bringing her here would be the last place they'd think of, so they won't look here. For all anyone knows she's still at the hangar at the airport. By the time anyone realizes differently we'll be long gone."

"So where are you going next?" Maitlyn asked, moving into the room behind them.

Kendrick tossed her a look but didn't bother to answer. His sister rolled her eyes.

Zak wrapped his arms around Maitlyn. "You know he can't say, Maitlyn."

"I can't say because right now I don't know," Kendrick said, his gaze flitting from one to the other. He shrugged his broad shoulders as his brow creased in thought.

"I have an idea," Maitlyn said. The two men eyed her curiously as she explained her plan.

Minutes later Kendrick said thoughtfully, "It's just crazy enough that it might work."

"I'm very good at what I do, little brother, and there haven't been too many problems that I've not been able to resolve."

Zak leaned back against the counter. "Honey, are you sure…" he started.

She leaned to kiss his cheek. "I'm positive. I think it's one of the best ideas I've had in a while."

Shrugging his shoulders, Zak wrapped her in a warm embrace as he rested his lips against her forehead. "Then let's do it," he said as he shot Kendrick a quick look.

Kendrick nodded. "I owe you," he said. "I owe you both."

Maitlyn eased out of her husband's arms. "You can trust I'll send you my bill," she said as she strolled out the door.

Kendrick laughed. "You can still get out of this," he teased. "It's not too late. Five more minutes though and I'm sure the fine print on that prenup she made you sign will kick in."

Zak laughed with him. "I'd be too scared," he teased back.

Chapter 4

"So what do you know about her?" Tarah Boudreaux asked her sister. She lifted her legs onto the mattress top, tucking them beneath her bottom.

Maitlyn shrugged her shoulders as their sister Kamaya pulled a brush through the length of her hair. "All I know is what Kendrick told me. She's a friend and she just stopped by to say hello to him. He's going to drop her off at the airport when he takes me and Zak to our plane."

"Since when does my twin bring a *friend* home?" Kamaya questioned, her eyebrows raised. She twisted a strand of Maitlyn's hair around a large-barreled curling iron.

"A friend with a baby," Tarah added.

Maitlyn shook her head. "It's not Kendrick's baby, so does it matter?"

Tarah pursed her lips in annoyance. "Are we sure about that?"

Maitlyn blew a deep sigh. "Tarah, you know good and well Kendrick is not that baby's father. Vanessa's not her mother. It's her cousin's baby or something. I don't know why you even want to go there."

"I'm just saying," Tarah intoned. "They both look a little too comfortable together if you ask me."

"Actually I think they're kind of cute together," Maitlyn mused. "I like her."

"I just find it strange that the first time he brings a *friend* home for us to meet it's at your wedding. This can't be casual," Kamaya said before standing back to stare at Maitlyn's head.

The three were interrupted by their mother, who peeked her head into the bedroom. "You girls need to stop gossiping about our company. Your daddy and I taught you better than that."

"We weren't gossiping," Tarah replied. "We just had some questions."

Katherine changed the subject. "Don't do her curls too tight, Kamaya. Maitlyn doesn't look right with tight curls."

"I know, Mama. They're going to fall some."

Katherine smiled. She moved to Maitlyn's side and leaned to kiss her daughter's cheek. "You were a beautiful bride today. Zakaria is a very lucky man."

Maitlyn nodded. "I think I might keep him," she said, joy glowing across her face.

"Mama, you don't think it's odd that Kendrick suddenly shows up with a woman and a baby we don't know anything about?"

"Tarah, you're about to work my last nerve," Katherine admonished. "Leave them two alone. If there was something Kendrick wanted us to know he would have told us."

Tarah crossed her arms over her chest. "You sure about that? 'Cause Kendrick is always keeping secrets!"

"Yes, I am." Katherine gave Tarah a light smack against her right thigh. "Now, mind your own business. If you spent as much time sweeping off your own porch you wouldn't have time to be sweeping off anyone else's."

"Ouch!" Taryn muttered, rubbing at the offending spot.

Maitlyn laughed. "Like she's ever listened before!"

"Tell me again why you got married before sunrise to hang out with your family all day afterward?" Tarah snapped.

Maitlyn laughed. "Tell me why you think everyone should do everything by the book? I had my dream wedding and there were some things I needed to get done before my husband and I disappear for a few days. It's all worked out perfectly."

Kamaya laughed. "Maitlyn took Senior's 'work before pleasure' rule literally!"

In the guest bedroom, Vanessa pulled her knees to her chest, curling her body around Gabi's. They had both been sleeping soundly when the sound of laughter pulled Vanessa from her sleep. Noise and laughter never seemed to stop ringing throughout the family's home and she couldn't miss hearing her name being spoken a time or two.

Kendrick had forewarned her about his sisters. Maitlyn being clued in had helped, the woman running interference when the other two had bombarded her with questions. Vanessa smiled.

She and Tarah were the same age, twenty-seven. They liked the same music, had shoe fetishes, dressed similarly, and both were in school working on advanced degrees. She imagined that if she were closer to her two brothers she would probably be the same way. But there was a considerable age difference between her and her siblings. It didn't help that both men had stayed in Mexico when their father was named ambassador to the United States, choosing not to move to Washington, DC, with the rest of the family. She didn't know enough about her brothers to be in their business that way. Tarah had the advantage there. Vanessa thought they could be good friends if things were different.

"If things were different" seemed to be a foregone conclusion to every thought she'd been having. If things were different, she might be able to relax and enjoy the family that was trying to make her feel comfortable. If things were different, she could flirt a little, or maybe even a lot, with the good-looking secret agent who was keeping a close eye on her. If things were different, she wouldn't feel so self-conscious, biting her tongue for fear of saying the wrong thing to the wrong person. But things weren't different and everything about where she was and what might happen to her was making her nervous.

Vanessa heaved a deep sigh, and then shifted her body from Gabi's. She knew the little girl would probably sleep for a good while but she was wide-awake and wanting answers about where they were headed next. Leaving the room door cracked in case Gabi woke and called out, Vanessa eased herself down the length of the hallway. Moving into the family's kitchen she wasn't expecting to turn and find the matriarch standing behind her. She jumped as she came face-to-face with the woman.

Katherine smiled brightly. "I didn't mean to scare you, baby. Would you like a cup of tea?"

Vanessa smiled and shook her head. "No, thank you, Mrs. Boudreaux. I do want to thank you for everything, though. You and your family have been really sweet."

Katherine nodded. "You are welcome here anytime. Any friend of Kendrick's is a friend of ours. It's too bad your bus didn't get here sooner so you could have made the wedding. It was a beautiful ceremony!" She moved to the other side of the center island as she lifted a teakettle onto the stove. "I peeked in on that sweet baby. Just as precious as she can be. And she's a handful! Little Miss Gabi has a lot of spirit."

Vanessa nodded. "She will definitely keep you on your toes," she answered.

"She's missing her mama. Hopefully she'll be able to get back to her soon."

Vanessa couldn't stop her eyes from misting with tears, suddenly wishing she could tell the kind woman

about her and Gabrielle's situation. Instead, she nodded, feeling even more awkward. "Do you know where
I might find your son?" she asked, needing to change
the subject.

"The men are all out on the patio," Katherine said,
pointing toward the outside.

Vanessa stood chewing on her bottom lip. She hated
feeling as if she was intruding, having no level of comfort to call on. The emotion was painted all over her face
and Katherine moved to ease her anxiety.

"Don't you worry about them boys," she said as she
gestured for Vanessa to follow her.

As they moved outdoors the men's conversation
came to an abrupt halt. They were engaged in a heated
debate about Miami versus New York in basketball.
Kendrick and Zak both turned to stare at her. His father,
Senior Boudreaux, gestured toward his wife. "Don't you
come out here fussin', woman!"

Katherine rolled her eyes as she moved to her husband's side, leaning to press her lips to his cheek. "No
one's fussing at you. Kendrick's friend was looking
for him."

"I didn't mean to interrupt," Vanessa said softly, her
eyes meeting Kendrick's.

"Pretty lady, you're not interrupting. We were just
talking basketball," Senior said.

Vanessa smiled. "Well, my money's on New York to
make the play-offs and take down Miami in the finals."

Senior jumped to his feet, throwing his hands into
the air. "That's what I'm talking about! What did I say
to you? Sounds like this lady knows her game!"

Kendrick and his brother Donovan jumped up with him. "There's no way they're going to take down Miami!" both exclaimed excitedly. "Not this year, or next year!"

Vanessa shrugged. "Miami's days are numbered. Just wait and see."

"How do you figure that?" Kendrick questioned. His eyes narrowed as he stared at her.

Vanessa moved toward him. "History."

"A history of getting beat," Kendrick intoned.

Vanessa smiled. "Not true. All of their matchups have been marked by aggressive play, defensive struggles, numerous foul calls and some intense physical play. You can trace that history back to Pat Riley and how he coached both teams back in the day. Both played hard and they went tit for tat. Now, granted, it took some serious reengineering of their roster to get New York back on point but this past year put them back on the map. They're a solid team and they're working together like a fine-oiled machine. They are going to serve them some serious game and I don't think Miami is going to be able to keep up. Besides, it's time they got their butts beat."

"Now I know you don't know what you're talking about," Kendrick exclaimed.

Vanessa smiled. "I bet you two courtside seats to a play-off game that I know exactly what I'm talking about."

Kendrick grinned. "I'll take that bet," he said, seemingly intrigued that she had the nerve to challenge him.

Her smiled widened, her gaze still locked with his.

There was a moment of pause as the family stood staring at them both.

Donovan interrupted the silence. "You need to check your girl, bro!"

Senior laughed. "I like you, little lady. School these youngsters!"

Katherine shook her head as she laughed with her husband. "Vanessa, as you can see, my boys take their sports very seriously."

Vanessa nodded, suddenly unnerved by the look Kendrick was giving her, his dark gaze seeming to strip her naked where she stood. She felt her breath catch in her throat. She was grateful when his mother distracted his attention away from her.

"I told Maitlyn you boys are waiting on her now. She said she'll be ready in about ten minutes. But, Zakaria, if you don't move that girl along you two are never going to get on that plane for your honeymoon," Katherine said as she took a quick glance down at her watch. "And I imagine Miss Vanessa and that sweet baby need to be headed to the bus station soon, too. Kendrick, did you put all the bags in the car?"

Kendrick and Zak exchanged a quick look. "Yes, ma'am," her son answered.

"Now, if you need to go on and take Vanessa, one of your brothers can run Zak and your sister to their plane."

Kendrick shook his head. "We're good. I can take them both."

Zak nodded. "And, if necessary, I can always arrange for a limo. But you know how Maitlyn is, Miss

Katherine. She'll just go with the flow. If things aren't perfect she will figure out a way to make them perfect."

Senior nodded. "It's a good thing she's spending your money, Zakaria. I'd be hot if she were spending my money!"

The men laughed as Katherine shook her head. "Well, we'll go check on her again and get everyone ready to say our goodbyes." She reached for her husband's hand and pulled him along behind her. "You all should come on in so we can give them a send-off," she said, tossing the comment over her shoulder as she and Senior moved back inside the home.

Zak came to his feet. "I'll see you two in a minute," he said as he followed behind his new in-laws.

"I guess I'll go, too," Donovan intoned.

And just like that Kendrick and Vanessa were surrounded by quiet, nothing but a low breeze blowing through the porch.

Vanessa wrapped her arms around her torso, hugging herself tightly. "I really like your family," she said, moving to take the seat his father had just vacated.

Kendrick nodded. "They're a good bunch," he responded, dropping down onto the cushion chair beside her. "So why were you looking for me?"

"I was hoping that you could tell me what's going to happen next? I know we can't stay here."

"No, we can't."

"So where are we going?"

"You really are a worrier, aren't you?"

"Don't I have reason to be?"

Kendrick shrugged his broad shoulders. "You really

can relax. You're going to be fine. I'm going to make sure of it. I promised you that."

Vanessa took a deep breath, holding it for a quick moment before she blew the warm air past her lips. Kendrick stared blankly at her again.

"What?" she said, catching his look.

Kendrick held up his hands. "Nothing. Sorry, I didn't mean to stare." He moved onto his feet. "We should go get Gabi ready. We need to leave soon," he said softly. Then without another word he turned and moved back into his family's home, leaving her sitting by her lonesome.

Vanessa sat in reflection for a few more minutes, staring at the late-afternoon sun as it began its slow descent in the bright blue sky. The days were starting to feel very long, one running right into the other. She had been able to sleep only in hourly increments since that night at the club when everything that could have gone wrong did. As the air cooled around her she suddenly felt as if time had come to a standstill and she was stuck in the midst of a tailspin with no way out. Inside, the family was consumed with joy and happiness, laughter ringing from room to room. In the midst of it she caught sight of Kendrick, little Gabrielle in his arms, her head resting against his shoulder. He didn't seem to have a care in the world. Rising to her feet, she moved inside to join them.

"What do you mean the baby's not going with us?" Vanessa snapped, her eyes darting from Kendrick to Zak and back. "Where is she going?"

"Zak and my sister are taking her to DC, to the Mexican embassy. The embassy is helping to find her grandparents and your mother has agreed to watch her until that happens."

"My mother? You spoke to my mother?"

"I did," Zak answered. "And we knew you were adamant about Gabi not going to a foster home, so your mother said they would ensure her safety at the embassy."

"Zak and I will make sure she's safe and sound until then," Maitlyn interjected as Gabi toyed with the pearl necklace around her neck.

Tears burned hot against her lids as Vanessa struggled not to cry. She didn't have the words to explain that Gabi was all she had left of a life that had once made sense. Gabrielle was her last connection to Alexandra and a friendship that had been her lifeline. Maitlyn moved to Vanessa's side and wrapped an arm around her shoulders.

"She's going to be just fine," Maitlyn assured her. "I promise."

Vanessa nodded. She pressed a kiss to Gabi's cheek and the little girl laughed, her hands clapping together excitedly as she pointed toward the luxury aircraft.

"'Pane!" Gabrielle squealed. "'Pane!"

"Airplane!" Vanessa said, forcing a bright smile onto her face. "Gabi's going to ride in the airplane."

"Gabi, 'pane?"

She nodded. "Yes. Gabrielle's going on the airplane. And you be a good girl for Auntie Nessa, okay? Auntie Nessa loves you, Gabi!"

Maitlyn gave Vanessa another warm hug. Kendrick moved to Vanessa's side as Zak escorted his new wife and the giggling little girl to the private aircraft. When the flight crew closed the door, the first of Vanessa's tears dripped past her lashes. As they stood inside the hangar watching the plane taxi out to the runway her tears rained heavy from her eyes. By the time the airplane was in the air she was inconsolable.

Vanessa found herself thinking back to that night when everything had gone bad. Rihanna had been blasting through the speakers and everyone was up on the dance floor. The pulsating rhythms through the nightclub had the place turned out. With her hands waving in the air above her head, she'd been gyrating to the beat, her body rocking from side to side on the dance floor. The Waterside Savoy, one of the premier nightclubs in the Miami area, catered to an elite clientele and Vanessa had been enjoying everything about the VIP treatment, thanks to her best friend, Alexandra, and her husband, Paolo Medina. It had been a while since Vanessa had last had such a good time and it didn't hurt that her date for the night was sexy as hell.

Marcus Bennett had been smitten and Vanessa had used that to her advantage, purposely flaunting her feminine wiles to get her way with the man. Since their initial introduction the four of them had lounged on the man's luxury yacht four days out of seven. Marcus had been the kind of man few women could resist. That night they'd been dancing cheek to cheek and the man had had her feeling all kinds of right. Then things changed.

Marcus had wrapped a tight arm around her slim waist and had pulled her closer to him. His mouth had trailed from her jawline to her ear. "Step away," he'd whispered as he'd given her a quick kiss on the cheek. "I need to handle some business."

Vanessa had eyed the stranger who'd walked up behind them, the man looking out of place on the dance floor. For a brief second she'd wanted to protest, the music feeling too good to stop. But the look in both of their eyes gave her reason to hesitate and so she nodded her head instead. Besides, she'd had to pee and that moment had been as good as any. As she'd headed in the direction of the ladies' room she had stopped to shimmy her hips beside Alexandra and Paolo, who were doing their own dirty shuffle in the middle of the crowd.

Alexandra had lifted her hands questioningly. "Where's Marcus?" she'd shouted over the loud clamor of the music.

"Business," Vanessa had shouted back with a quick shrug of her shoulders.

Paolo and Alexandra had turned to stare where she pointed. When Paolo bristled, suddenly moving in his friend's direction, the two women had tossed each other a look. Concern had blanketed Alexandra's face. The look in her eyes still haunted Vanessa.

She'd turned toward the ladies' room, gesturing for her friend to follow, but Alexandra had refused, shaking her head no. "I just fought that crowd," she'd said. "I think I'll go back to the table and order us all another round of drinks."

"Shots!" Vanessa remembered exclaiming. "Let's do chocolate cake shooters!"

Alexandra had laughed, the last time Vanessa would ever see her best friend so happy. Then she'd turned around, following behind her husband.

As Vanessa had moved toward the bathroom the music shifted to a slow jam, the DJ spinning something relaxed and easy. The first gunshot silenced the sounds to a dull drone, as everyone seemed to hold their collective breaths. When Vanessa turned to look, someone shrieked. Then madness ensued. There was a frenzied rush for the doors, people screaming and yelling as shot after shot echoed around them. A man standing beside her had pushed Vanessa down to the ground, dropping harshly against her as the crowd scurried like roaches around them. Her face had slammed into the floor and she'd tasted blood when her teeth bit down against her bottom lip. The moment was surreal and when the clouds cleared, the last thing Vanessa remembered was Marcus Bennett turning an about-face in the doorway, his pistol still in his hand.

Vanessa shook her head, consumed by the memory as it filled her with emotion. Kendrick let her cry, wrapping his arms around her torso and pulling her to his chest. She sobbed into the front of his shirt and when she was all cried out, the last of her sobs shifting into sniffles, he was still holding tightly to her.

Chapter 5

"So, where are we now?" Vanessa questioned, swiping the sleep from her eyes. The private jet had landed just minutes earlier and was taxiing to a slow halt. Vanessa peered out the plane's window, nothing about the landscape recognizable.

Kendrick met the look she was giving him, her eyebrows arched questioningly.

"Pleasure Island," he responded.

"Pleasure Island?"

He nodded. "We commandeered Maitlyn and Zak's honeymoon. No one will think to look for us here."

Vanessa's eyes widened. "Their honeymoon? We can't take their honeymoon!" she exclaimed.

Kendrick shrugged. "It's no big deal. Besides, it was my sister's idea. She and Zak should be headed to Tahiti in the next hour or so after they drop off the kid. They won't be missing out."

Vanessa blew a deep sigh. "That kid has a name," she said, annoyance pulling at her expression.

He smiled. "Sorry… After they leave Gabrielle with your mother they plan to honeymoon on the Polynesian Islands."

There was a moment of pause as Vanessa took in the news. "I don't have any clothes," she said, the thought suddenly distressing her.

"It's been taken care of. Maitlyn made some calls. You'll have everything you need."

She finally nodded. "So what do you know about this place?" she questioned, trying to recall everything she'd ever read about the luxury vacation spot.

Kendrick shrugged. "All I know is it's expensive. My new brother-in-law has some deep pockets."

"It's a little more than that," she said, suddenly remembering that Pleasure Island was an infamous couples-only retreat. Catering to an exclusive clientele, the all-inclusive resort was renowned for its secluded location, gourmet dining and 24/7 service and amenities. "I think I read somewhere that Jay-Z and Beyoncé come here every few months to keep the zing in their relationship," she said matter-of-factly.

"Really?" Kendrick said with a deep laugh. "I'll have to ask him about it the next time we shoot hoops."

Vanessa's expression was blank as she stared at him. She rolled her eyes. "You really don't expect me to believe that you play ball with Jay-Z?"

He shrugged, his broad shoulders tensing slightly.

"If you act right I might take you along the next time we get together."

Vanessa's expression remained unmoved. She shook her head. "It's your lie. Tell it anyway you want," she said.

Kendrick laughed again. "Okay, whatever." He changed the subject. "This is what's going to happen. We're checking in as the newly married Mr. and Mrs. Sayed. Call me *honey*, I'll call you *baby*, and neither of us will need to worry about remembering our fake names. You relax in the sun by the pool, I'll do a little fishing, and in a few days I'll escort you back to the States. You'll testify and then I'll take you home. Until then, I promise not to bite as long as you don't." He chuckled softly.

Vanessa stared at him, finding nothing to laugh about. He moved from his seat into the cockpit to speak with the pilot. There was something about the way he carried himself that unnerved her. His nonchalant attitude also prickled her nerves. But his gaze was soothing, like a warm blanket on a chilly night. He had beautiful eyes and she imagined many a woman had gotten herself lost in them. And then there was that damn smile.

He made everything sound so easy, as if they were doing nothing more than taking a short stroll down a long street. But despite his best efforts she was still filled to her limit with anxiety. The way her stomach was doing flips she sensed there wasn't going to be anything easy about being stranded on a seductive island with the likes of Kendrick Boudreaux.

* * *

Pleasure Island was the epitome of luxury. Renowned for its ambience, the romantic island resort was living up to its reputation and they'd barely been there for an hour. The outdoor landscape was full and lush, bright green fronds skirting the endless water views. There was an abundance of exotic flora that scented the air and Vanessa stopped to sniff the hibiscus.

As she stared about, awed by their surroundings, Kendrick stepped back to watch her. There was something in her demeanor that he found intriguing. He found himself smiling as he watched the tension that had once furrowed her brow begin to slowly fade away. Her apprehensive expression shifted and he could almost see the weight of her circumstances being lifted off her shoulders. She suddenly looked in his direction and tossed him an easy smile before dipping her nose back into a sweet bouquet of orchids, cyclamen, tulips and anemones, the bright hues seeming to soothe her spirit.

Their private bungalow was at the far end of the resort. Inside, the decor was upscale and inviting. Sliding glass doors led to a secluded terrace with a hot tub and their own infinity pool. In the distance a stone-paved path led to an expanse of white sand. A pristine shoreline kissed the bright blue water on the private beach and they could see the sun starting to descend in the distance. It was the Garden of Eden in all its glory.

From the moment the duo was escorted to their suite, the experience was meant to tempt and satisfy their sensual pleasures and afford them the opportunity to explore and indulge all of their sexual fantasies. Every wish and desire could be entertained, from the most romantic to the most hedonistic.

The brochure encouraged whatever pleasures one could imagine. There were the "nude" and "prude" beaches, never-ending food and drink, massages and clothing-optional activities. And enclosed behind a decorative door in the tiled bathroom was a vending machine filled with erotic toys. As Vanessa stood staring at the vast selection she shook her head. There were some things inside that Vanessa couldn't even begin to imagine.

"You said your sister picked this place out?" Vanessa questioned, cutting an eye in his direction as she moved back into the room where Kendrick sat. She walked to the other end of the sofa and plopped down.

"Yeah. Zak didn't even know where they were going."

Vanessa nodded. *I think your sister's a freak,* she thought to herself as she scanned the welcome brochure they'd been given at check-in. The four-page pamphlet read like a grocery list of all things decadent.

As if reading her mind Kendrick spoke the thought out loud. "I think my sister has some issues!" he said as he eyed his own brochure.

Vanessa laughed. "It *was* supposed to be their honeymoon," she said, still giggling.

"There are some things about my sisters that I just don't need to know."

Moving back onto her feet Vanessa crossed the front

living space into the oversize bedroom. Kendrick followed behind her. Glass encased the room on three sides and a king-size bed sat in the room's center, offering extraordinary water views on one side and exquisite garden views on the other. The bedding was an exquisite blend of silks and satins with a wealth of pillows that beckoned one beneath the sheets.

Both Vanessa and Kendrick spoke at the same time. "I'll take the bedroom."

She cut an eye in his direction. "Yes, I will," she said, a hint of attitude in her tone. She eyed him with a raised brow. The look she gave him challenged him to contradict her.

Kendrick snapped his finger, feigning disappointment. "I guess that means I'm sleeping on the couch."

"That's exactly what that means." Vanessa moved to the bedside and threw her body against the mattress. Her arms were extended out to her sides and she lifted both of her legs in the air as she crossed her ankles one over the other. She bent her legs at the knees and lifted her torso slightly as she adjusted the pillows beneath her head. "A girl could get used to this," she muttered as she relaxed into the comfort.

Amusement painted Kendrick's expression. "I'm sure a guy could get used to it, too!" he said.

Vanessa leaned up on her elbow to stare at him. A slight smile pulled at his full lips. The intense stare he was giving her was intoxicating. As she eyed him from head to toe a wave of heat flushed her cheeks. For a brief moment, there was invitation in her eyes and she knew it. She was unable to control the wanting that suddenly swept through her. She bit down against her bottom lip and dropped her gaze to the bedspread.

"Maybe we can share," she said after a brief moment of thought. "I'll get the bed tonight, maybe tomorrow, too. Then you can sleep here one night after that."

Kendrick chuckled. "You sound very convincing," he said, the words edged in sarcasm.

A bright smile filled her face as she shrugged her shoulders. "You say that like you don't believe me."

"I don't."

Kendrick was caught off guard as she met the look he was giving her with one of her own. Her eyes were narrowed ever so slightly as she appraised him. There was something curious in her stare. He suddenly turned and moved out of the room. As he'd stood watching her, heat had coursed through his loins. He could feel the beginnings of an erection pulling at his muscles and he knew that only distance would make the sensation go away. He took a deep breath and then a second. When he heard her moving behind him he hurried down the hallway and back into the living space.

As he moved into the room there was an abrupt knock at the door that distracted them both. Kendrick took three quick strides to the other side of the room. He hesitated for a brief moment, his hand on the doorknob. Vanessa had moved to the entranceway, peering out. The two locked gazes for a brief moment before he opened the door.

The man standing on the other side was grinning broadly. He was exceptionally short, standing well below Kendrick's six feet three inches. He had bright blue eyes and thick blond curls. He wore a white linen suit, a white dress shirt open at the collar and white canvas shoes. He stood with a bottle of champagne in an ice bucket, a white towel folded over his forearm.

"Welcome, sir! My name is Liam. I will be your butler for the duration of your stay."

Kendrick nodded. "Nice to meet you, Liam." He took a step back to let the man inside.

Liam nodded in Vanessa's direction. "Madam, welcome!"

Vanessa smiled, tilting her head slightly, but she said nothing.

"You requested *Domaine Carneros*. This is the Brut Rosé Sparkling Wine that you asked for." He moved to the bungalow's bar and set the ice bucket atop the wooden counter. He looked to Kendrick for direction. "Would you like for me to pour for you, sir?"

Kendrick shook his head. "I appreciate the offer, Liam, but I think I can handle it."

"Yes, sir. If there is anything you or your bride needs I am just a call away," Liam said.

Kendrick nodded. "We appreciate that."

"Will you be dining in tonight, sir? Or would you like to be seated in the dining room?"

Kendrick hesitated for a split second as he tossed Vanessa a look. She shrugged as he deferred the question to her.

"Can we dine on the beach?" she asked softly.

"Not a problem, madam," Liam replied, his full grin a mile wide. "I'll take care of everything."

Kendrick opened the door as Liam moved back through it. "Just push the red button on the phone, sir. That will reach me directly," he said as he made his exit.

"A butler bearing champagne!" Kendrick exclaimed when the door was closed shut behind the man.

"Your sister has great taste," Vanessa said as she inspected the vintage bottle of spirits. "Do you want a glass?"

Kendrick shook his head. "Sorry, I don't drink when I'm on duty."

Vanessa shrugged. "Suit yourself," she said as she popped the cork and poured herself a full glass. She took her first sip and smiled.

Kendrick shook his head. "And why the beach? We could have eaten in the dining room."

Vanessa tossed him a look as she grabbed the wine bottle and her glass and turned back in the direction of the bedroom. "It's our wedding night, remember? I didn't think it would look very convincing if we were sitting in a public place scowling at each other," she said.

As she disappeared from view, Kendrick chuckled softly. "I don't think you'd be scowling," he mumbled under his breath.

You could see the tent and table from the patio. Kendrick had taken a shower and a nap and had already moved outside, staring down to where Liam and the staff were setting up on the beach. He watched as they put up a bamboo canopy and draped it with a white gauze fabric. Then they moved a table and two chairs beneath it. Large tiki lights were propped strategically around the beach front and the dining area was dressed in white linens and the resort's signature china. As the sun was beginning to set off in the distance Vanessa stepped past the sliding glass doors and joined him.

He turned to stare as she moved to his side. She'd changed into a pale blue slip dress, the hem skirting inches above her knees. The fabric was sheer and when the light caught her at the right angle he could see the outline of her body, nothing else between the garment and her skin.

"Are you wearing anything under that dress?" he asked as he forced himself to look into her eyes.

Vanessa laughed. "Do you always get so personal with your clients?"

Embarrassment flushed Kendrick's cheeks, deepening his complexion a rich shade of red. "I didn't mean to say that out loud."

"I'm on my honeymoon, remember," Vanessa said, her tone teasing. "I imagine I wouldn't be wearing a lot of clothes on my honeymoon. Besides, your sister didn't give me a whole lot to work with."

"Even if you were on your honeymoon there are staff at these resorts who might see you."

She giggled. "I don't think Liam minds what he sees. But if you're a little sensitive about it, *darling*, I'll try to put more on next time."

Kendrick crossed his arms over his chest. "I think you might be taking this pretend thing a little far," he said.

"Maybe. Maybe not." Vanessa laughed and shrugged.

"But I didn't pick out the wardrobe, remember? Besides, you're one to talk, standing there half-naked yourself!"

She eyed him from head to toe. He was bare-chested and barefoot, wearing nothing but a pair of tan linen slacks. His upper body was chiseled, every muscle rock-hard and perfect. Standing there staring at her, he looked like a fitness model flexing his pecs, biceps and picture-perfect, six-pack abs.

"Agent Boudreaux, if I have to be kept prisoner, I plan to enjoy it," she said. "Now, let's get dinner, *husband.* I'm hungry."

Kendrick shook his head, feeling slightly deviant as he found himself wondering what she might feel like in his arms. He imagined his hands stealing beneath that sheer dress to tease her skin and trailing his fingers across her sweet spots. Heat rushed from one end of his body to the other and he was suddenly grateful for the easy breeze blowing off the ocean waters. He followed behind her as she led the way down to the beach.

Liam greeted them warmly. "Welcome, madam. Welcome, sir. I hope everything meets with your approval?"

Vanessa's eyes widened with wonder. "Everything is beautiful!" she exclaimed as she took in the view. "Isn't it beautiful?" she said as she tossed Kendrick a quick look.

Kendrick nodded. "Thank you, Liam," he said as the man pulled out a chair for Vanessa to take a seat.

When they both were seated comfortably, the butler filled their empty water glasses. Vanessa requested wine with her food, but Kendrick passed. The meal started with a salad of mixed greens, beets, mango, red bell peppers and yellow tomatoes tossed with cracked pepper, sea salt and a macadamia nut vinaigrette. Dinner was a seafood special of ahi sashimi, sweet lobster cake with a jalapeno and mango chutney, and grilled prawns with a truffle and soy dipping sauce. The meal was beyond delicious, satiating all of their senses.

Vanessa licked her fingers, remnants of the truffle sauce dotting the tips. She sucked her index finger past her full lips then slowly pulled it from her mouth. The erotic gesture caught Kendrick's attention and as he watched her, his entire body froze, his muscles tensing. She suddenly lifted her eyes to his and his breath caught deep in his chest. He took a deep breath of air and then another, fighting to look everywhere but at her.

"Sorry." Vanessa giggled. "That wasn't very lady-like, was it?"

Kendrick shrugged. "Clearly, you enjoyed your meal." Amusement danced around the edges of his dark eyes and his tone was teasing.

She giggled. "Like you've never licked your fingers before!" She shifted forward in her seat as he dipped his last prawn in the decadent sauce and drew it to his full lips. She reached for the cloth napkin and extended it toward him. Her grin was miles wide as her eyes dared him to take it from her hand.

His own smile spread slowly as he looked at her. He reached for the napkin with his left hand as he slowly sucked one finger and then another from his right hand into his mouth. When he'd washed all five digits with his tongue, he swiped the cloth over his hands before dropping it into his empty plate. "The food was good!" he said, glancing at Vanessa. She seemed to be holding her breath as she watched him.

"It was divine!" she exclaimed as she reached for her wineglass, savoring the last sip. "Absolutely divine!"

There was a moment of quiet between them as they paused to watch the light shimmer against the water. Small waves broke along the shoreline, the tranquil sound soothing. The temperature was perfect, stars danced in the clear sky overhead and the moon was casting just enough light to give the darkness around them a seductive ambience. Kendrick imagined that for those couples who were honeymooning, Pleasure Island couldn't have been more perfect.

Minutes passed before either spoke, Kendrick finally breaking the silence. 'It's good to see you relax at last," he said.

Vanessa smiled, an easy bend to her mouth that moved him to smile back. "This is the first time I've felt safe since…" She hesitated, meeting his gaze for a quick second before dropping her eyes. She took a deep breath before venturing to look back at him. "I feel safe and comfortable. I haven't felt this way in a long time, even before all this mess happened."

Kendrick nodded, turning to stare back at the ocean.

"I imagine your girlfriend isn't happy about you being here," Vanessa said, eyeing him curiously.

"I don't have a girlfriend."

"Your boyfriend, then."

He laughed. "Not that it's any of your business but

I don't date men. Why are you fishing for information about my personal life?"

She laughed with him. "Well, since I didn't see a ring on your hand I didn't want to assume you had a wife."

"Well, I don't have either, a wife or a girlfriend. This isn't the type of job that's conducive to a relationship."

"Is that why Zak isn't your partner anymore? Your sister said you two used to be partners."

"We were. Now he wants to focus his time and energy on being a good husband."

"What about you? Would you give this up for a woman?"

Kendrick met the intense stare she was giving him as he reflected on her question. "She would have to be a very special woman," he finally said.

She was still staring at him when Liam came rushing down the path, interrupting the moment.

"Sir, madam, dessert has been set up in your bungalow. Whenever you two are ready." He gestured in the direction of their quarters.

Kendrick turned to Vanessa. She seemed as confused as he was.

Liam grinned. "Madam ordered the Honeymoon Special to be served in the bedroom when your reservations were made."

Vanessa's eyes widened. "Oh…yes…I did…didn't I…" she stammered.

Liam didn't look fazed as he gestured with his hand a second time.

"Madam is full of surprises," Kendrick said as he

rose from his seat. He moved around the table to pull out Vanessa's chair. "Shall we, my dear?"

"Why, thank you, honey!"

Reaching for her hand, Kendrick entwined her fingers between his own as he pulled her along beside him. Behind them, Liam wished them both a good-night, then proceeded to clear the table. Kendrick and Vanessa both tossed the man one last look before closing the sliding glass doors behind them.

Inside, it looked as if hundreds of candles had been lit, the room glowing from the multitude of wax pillars that decorated the space. A trail of rose petals led from the living room to the bedroom. Curiosity pulled them both down the short length of hallway to peek inside.

A silver tray sat in the center of the bed. It held a decadent four-layer slice of cheesecake decorated with berries, chocolate shavings and mint. The serving was lavish and meant to be shared, as evidenced by the single spoon resting along its side.

Kendrick suddenly realized he was still holding tight to her hand.

Vanessa cut an eye in his direction. "It's only pretend, right?" She lifted both their intertwined hands upward.

He tossed his head back and laughed heartily.

Laughing with him Vanessa kicked off her shoes and moved to the bed. Climbing atop the covers she moved to the center, sitting Indian-style before the tray. She reached for the spoon as she gave him another look. "I have a serious sweet tooth," she said nonchalantly.

Still chuckling Kendrick shook his head. "Half of that is mine," he said as he took a seat beside her, grabbing the spoon from her hands. He bumped his shoulder against hers, the gesture meant to be playful. He wasn't expecting the sudden rush of heat that shot through his body, an electrical current coursing through every nerve ending. It caught him off guard and in that split second, Vanessa hijacked the spoon.

Chapter 6

Kendrick had wakened with a smile on his face. He was still grinning from ear to ear as he took one last lap across the beach and around the path Liam had laid out for him. He'd risen early and the weather had been perfect for an early-morning run. It felt good to stretch his legs and warm his muscles. He and Vanessa had talked until well past the midnight hour. Sharing that dessert had ignited a level of friendship between them that neither had expected, most especially after he'd been able to snag the only spoon. They'd both been relaxed and had laughed and joked about absolutely nothing.

As he came to an abrupt stop, his lungs burned. He leaned forward, both hands resting against his thighs as he fought to catch his breath. The warm air felt good and although the sand had challenged his long legs, the run had done him good. He stood upright, admiring the new-day sun as it rose into the crisp blue sky. Shifting up and down on his toes he waved his arms back and forth pumping blood into his extremities. All the while he was still thinking about Vanessa and the night they'd shared.

There was something about her that he liked. She had an air of maturity that belied her youthful exuberance. He sensed that much like his sister Tarah she wasn't yet ready to grow up and assume the adult title even though she was one. And just like Tarah, being the baby in her family, she was spoiled rotten.

The dessert they'd shared had led to a conversation about food, which had turned into a discussion about their favorite things to do, ending with them laughing hysterically over past antics. He'd revealed to her some things he'd never before shared with anyone. She had told on herself a few times, as well.

Reflecting on that Kendrick was surprised by how easy she'd been to talk to. And how easy she was on the eyes. The woman was intoxicatingly beautiful. It had been easy to ignore his own body's persistent reaction to the closeness of her while they'd been playful but he imagined that if she spent any more time half-dressed, that might become more difficult to do. He was attracted to her and he couldn't be, and more important, he definitely couldn't let her know what he was feeling. He took a deep breath in, shaking his head as he pondered his options.

* * *

There was no answer when Vanessa called Kendrick's name. She'd been alone when she finally managed to open her eyes. Sunlight was streaming through the glass enclosure and she could hear the lull of the seawater through the screened doors. She'd woken to rose petals tangled through her hair and her crotch and the memory of her night with Kendrick stuck in her head. The man had haunted her dreams and waking to thoughts of him had her feeling some kind of way. She'd called out for him and when there'd been no answer she'd risen from the mattress to search him out.

She liked Kendrick. She hated to admit it but there was something about him that moved her spirit. She felt safe with him and that allowed her to let her guard down. They'd spent hours talking over that sweet piece of cheesecake and she'd been comfortable opening up to him. He'd teased her and she hadn't felt self-conscious once. He made her laugh and it felt natural to do so. And despite his kindness toward her, he seemed indifferent to her feminine wiles, never blinking once when she'd tried to be flirtatious.

She looked out to the beach and saw him standing at the water's edge. He appeared to be deep in thought, his focus someplace else. Once again, he was shirtless, his broad back rippling with muscle upon muscle. This time he was wearing swim trunks and his long legs were solid as tree trunks. Vanessa took a deep breath. Any other time, any other place, and she wouldn't have given a single thought to resisting the temptation sweeping through her. But this was the wrong time and the wrong place and clearly, he wasn't thinking the same things about her that she was thinking about him. Blowing a low sigh she headed for the bathroom and a very cold shower.

"What are you drinking?" Vanessa asked when she finally joined Kendrick on the patio. He was sipping a neon-green concoction through a straw.

"Vegetable juice. This one is kale, celery, spinach, apples and an orange. Have some?"

Vanessa skewed her face in distaste. "No, thank you. I want a real breakfast." She suddenly jumped when Liam moved to her side to take her order.

"Good morning, madam!"

Her eyes were wide as she shot the man a look. "Liam, you scared me!" she gushed, a hand pressed to her chest. "I wasn't expecting you to be there. Good morning."

"My apologies, madam. I definitely didn't mean to frighten you." He swept an apologetic look from Vanessa to Kendrick and back. "What might I get you for breakfast this morning?"

Vanessa pondered the question. "I'll have two eggs over easy, whole wheat toast, bacon—extra crispy— and a large glass of orange juice, please."

The man nodded. "I'll bring that right out," he said, disappearing as quickly as he'd appeared.

"Doesn't that make you nervous?" she asked, tossing Kendrick a look.

"What?"

"The way he just shows up out of the blue."

"It's his job. He does it well."

"He's creepy."

"Would you like me to ask them for someone else?"

She shook her head. "No. If he tries anything I think I can take him. He's not that big."

Kendrick laughed, tossing his head back against his shoulders. "I'd actually pay to see that."

"I wasn't trying to be funny. I'm dead serious."

"I'm sure you are," Kendrick answered. "But if it really makes you uncomfortable there's a do-not-disturb sign that you can hang on the door. He won't enter as long as that sign is up." He took another sip of his freshly squeezed juice.

"Is there a reason you're not eating real food?" Vanessa questioned. "Are you some kind of health nut?"

"Eating healthy doesn't mean I'm a nut. I just like to watch what I put into my body. You should try it."

"There's nothing wrong with my body," Vanessa said as she moved onto her feet to give him a little spin.

"It's all right," he muttered, feigning disinterest.

Vanessa rolled her eyes. Before she could respond Liam suddenly reappeared with her food and a large bowl of freshly cut fruit for Kendrick. He then excused himself, vanishing one more time. She shook her head.

"So, what's on our agenda today?" she questioned as she took a bite out of the toasted bread.

"I guess we're still honeymooning, or at least pretending to be. What do couples do on their honeymoon?"

She gave him a wry look. "Really? You're asking me that?"

He shrugged, a grin pulling at his full lips. "What? I've never been on a honeymoon before. And I bet you can't think of five things you'd do if you really were."

She shook her head. "What are you wagering?"

"Excuse me?"

"You want to bet me. What are you wagering?"

A slow smile pulled at Kendrick's mouth. "Whatever you want," he finally answered.

Vanessa smiled back. She dropped her fork onto her plate and sat back against her cushioned seat. She held up her hand and began to count out a list.

"First, I'd record every minute because someday the footage would make a spectacular movie for our grandchildren. I'm a film student, you know. I imagine we'd take long walks and just talk about our goals. There would be a lot of hand-holding and kisses and just easy, gentle touches. We would skinny-dip at least once, maybe twice. Then of course there'd be great sex. My husband and I would have really great sex. Really great sex all over the place."

"That's not five things."

"Yes, it is."

"No, it isn't. The hand-holding, kissing, touching and great sex are all one thing. You'd have great sex and make a porn movie for everyone to talk about."

"I would *not* make a porn movie."

"You would if you're having all that sex and filming while you do."

Vanessa rolled her eyes as Kendrick continued.

"And you might as well toss skinny-dipping in there, too, since you'd be naked."

"Skinny-dipping is not sex. I'm sure it could lead to sex but…"

Kendrick laughed. "Okay. So, you'll make a movie, have sex, skinny-dip, have sex and then have lots more sex. I think you're a little sex-obsessed."

"It is my honeymoon!" she said sarcastically. "Plus, there'd be long walks, too. Then more sex!"

"That's still only four."

Vanessa paused for a brief moment. "And we would pray together," she said. "That's five."

"Finally, something that doesn't have to do with sex."

"The Bible does say go forth and multiply."

Kendrick shook his head, clearly amused by the wide grin she was giving him. "Definitely obsessed," he muttered.

"Do you want me to keep going?"

"No. I have no doubts it would have something to do with sex."

Vanessa laughed. "My husband won't have a problem with that. He'll be a very lucky man."

Kendrick eyed the smirk on her face. His head was still moving from side to side. "So, what did you win? What am I going to have to give you?"

Her eyes narrowed ever so slightly. "Let me think about it," she said. "I'll let you know at dinner tonight."

He shrugged as he took the last bite of his fruit salad, avoiding the look she was giving him. "What?" he finally asked.

"So, really," she persisted, "what are we going to do today?"

* * *

Vanessa stepped into the heated shower to rinse the sand and salt water from her skin. The warm water felt good, the massage showerhead invigorating to her flesh. It had been a long day and she was physically exhausted. Asking Kendrick what was on the agenda had sounded good hours ago but she hadn't been prepared for the workout he'd put her through.

After they were done with breakfast they'd gone out to explore the resort. On the public side of their bungalow were the resort's two larger pools, one nestled beneath a canopy of shade trees. The water was clear and warm and only a handful of vacationers sat poolside. Kendrick had insisted on swimming a few laps and she had watched him, her body extended across one of the lounge chairs as she bathed in the sun. Watching him was quickly becoming her favorite new hobby.

Just minutes from their secluded and quiet retreat were bustling bars, upscale restaurants and designer boutiques. They'd entertained themselves exploring each shop and Vanessa quickly discovered that his tastes were not far from her own. She'd taken much joy in pretending to shop for their fake home back in the States. She'd put on quite a performance for the shopkeepers. It had thrown him the first time, maybe even the second, but by the third time he was rolling the story with her.

On the open beach couples were playing volleyball, the men against the women. Kendrick had insisted they join in. The fun and games had been a good time right up to the moment someone had slammed the volleyball against the side of her head. As she'd put up her hand, hoping to defer the strike, she'd broken two nails. Holding up her hands beneath the water raining over her shoulders, the memory of the incident annoyed her.

They'd grabbed lunch at one of the many buffets set up in the public areas and once she'd feasted on her meal of crab-stuffed fish fillets, Kendrick had been ready to move on. They'd hiked through the lush landscape, stopping only once to enjoy an icy beverage of ginger and pureed strawberry juice over crushed ice. Then he'd spotted the watercrafts. They'd spent the rest of the afternoon on Jet Skis, racing each other on the open waterways. Now she was exhausted, wanting only to catch a quick nap before dinner. She groaned in fatigue as she rinsed the last of the suds from her skin. Stepping out of the tiled enclosure she wrapped a bright white towel around her body. She moved to the sink and brushed her teeth, polishing them to a pearly shine. Once she moisturized her face and slathered her body with coconut oil she moved back into the bedroom and tossed her body down against the mattress top. Seconds later Vanessa was sound asleep.

Kendrick could hear Vanessa snoring softly from his resting spot in the living room. He smiled, grateful that he was finally able to get a much-needed break. They'd been going full steam since earlier that morning and he'd done everything in his power to keep them both occupied and busy. Spending time with the beautiful woman was more of a challenge than he'd imagined. She excited him and her flirtatious manner continued to catch him off guard. Vanessa could be a tease and she would purposely do things to make him blush, enjoying those moments when she could get a rise out of him. Literally. Maintaining some distance had become a serious necessity. He exhaled a gust of warm breath past his full lips. With any luck she would sleep until morning. Tomorrow was another day and he was already plotting what he might do to keep her occupied.

There was a light knock at the door and he lifted his body, crossing the floor quickly to pull it open. Liam stood on the other side. Kendrick drew his index finger to his lips and stepped outside, closing the door behind them.

The butler held out a Globalstar satellite telephone. "It's Sayed," the man said.

Kendrick nodded as Liam stepped off to the side, ensuring no one else could hear the conversation.

"How's that honeymoon going?" Zak asked, the hint of a laugh in his tone.

Kendrick chuckled softly. "More of a challenge than I thought it would be."

"You're a professional. You can handle it."

"Last week I would have agreed with you."

"Your sister never does anything without a reason. You know that, right?"

"And you're telling me this why?"

"Just thought you might like to know she set you up. It seems like your witness made quite an impression. Even your mother liked her."

Kendrick grunted in exasperation. "Well, you and I both know nothing can happen between us. Vanessa

Harrison is off-limits." He changed the subject. "So, how are things on your end?"

"The little girl was delivered safely. I also made sure everything else was put into place."

"So now we wait. And if I'm right, we won't have to wait too long."

"Are you sure there aren't any loose ends we need to worry about?"

Kendrick shook his head. "No, everything's good. You go enjoy your honeymoon. To hear Vanessa tell it, *you'll* get to have a *really* good time."

Zak laughed. "Life's short, my friend. Don't let it pass you by."

"And your point?"

"Don't do anything I wouldn't do."

"This coming from the man who seduced my sister while he was on a mission?"

"This coming from the man who fell in love with the woman of his dreams while he was on a mission."

Kendrick nodded into the receiver. "Tell that woman she doesn't play fair. She could have packed the girl some real clothes!"

His brother-in-law laughed. "I will. You stay safe," Zak said as he disconnected the line.

Kendrick held the receiver for a moment as he reflected on his friend's words. Despite his sister's wishful thinking he wasn't willing to ignore his responsibilities or jeopardize Vanessa's safety. Maybe the woman did excite him. And maybe if things were different he might be willing to see what could develop between them. But there was nothing he could even think about doing until they apprehended Marcus Bennett and she was able to testify. He turned as Liam moved back to his side.

"How come you always get the cushy assignments?" Liam asked as he took the radio back from his associate.

"It really isn't all it's cracked up to be," Kendrick said.

Liam smirked. "Yeah, right! You get to babysit a beautiful, half-naked woman while I serve chips and dip. I'll trade places with you any day of the week."

Kendrick laughed. "Good night, Liam."

"Right back atcha, boss!"

Kendrick eased back inside the bungalow. It was eerily quiet and then he heard Vanessa snore, and knew sleep still claimed her. Moving stealth-like down the hall to the bedroom, he eased open the door and peeked inside. The young woman lay facedown against the still-made bed, a white towel wrapped around her body. Her bare legs peeked out from beneath the square of fabric, the fabric barely covering her assets. She looked almost angelic lying there and Kendrick had to force himself to step back out of the room, thinking he could easily spend hours watching her as she slept.

Easing the door closed he moved back to the living room and stretched his body across the sofa. He knew that it wouldn't be long before he would be sound asleep himself. But as he lay there he found himself actually missing Vanessa, wishing they were still side by side laughing about something silly. He enjoyed those moments when everything around them was forgotten and it was just the two of them focused intently on each other. He had never known that kind of connection with a woman before. He had never before been in a position where he had the time or the ability to get to know any woman that well. But he was getting to know much about the beautiful woman in the other room. And everything he was discovering he liked very much.

Tossing a hand over his eyes he knew there were questions he still needed to ask. He still needed to know more about her and her boyfriend. He needed to know if Vanessa was missing the man. If her loyalty to Marcus Bennett was greater than the interest she might have in him. If the level of comfort between them was what it seemed or if he was just wishing it into being. And even more than the questions he had for her, Kendrick realized there were things he needed to be asking himself.

They were only days away from the holiday season and he'd been thinking about his family. He marveled at the relationship between Zak and his sister; how easily they found balance with each other. He had never seen either of them happier until they'd met and he often wondered if he would ever find that kind of love for himself, if he even wanted it; a thought Vanessa suddenly had him reconsidering. He had become comfortable with the uncertainty in his life. Never knowing from day to day where God would lead him. Grateful that in those moments when there was a challenge tossed his way that his decisions affected only him. But he couldn't help speculating if there was something else waiting for him. Was there someone meant to share his destiny?

His parents and siblings would all be together for Thanksgiving and Christmas. He had nieces and nephews who barely knew him and that disturbed him. His brief time with little Gabi had him rethinking his own feelings about having children, had him wondering if he could be half the parent his own father had been. He also couldn't help but ponder about the woman who might bear his child. What about her would let him know that she was the one?

For the first time in a long time Kendrick found himself unable to focus, too much running through his mind. The situation he was suddenly thrust into had him wanting things he had never considered before. The holiday season made him sentimental and like too many years before, he didn't know if he would be there to celebrate with his family. Or if he would still be lost in paradise with Vanessa.

Chapter 7

The sun was just beginning to rise when Vanessa opened her eyes. She stretched her body outward, extending her arms over her head and her legs off the bed. Sitting upright she realized she was still wrapped in the white towel from her late-evening shower. And she was hungry, having missed the previous night's dinner.

In the distance she could hear Kendrick having a conversation with someone and she couldn't begin to imagine who he could be talking to. She reached for her wristwatch, which rested on the nightstand. It was well after eight o'clock in the morning. She shook her head, surprised that she had slept so intensely and for so long. She moved to the bathroom to wash her face and brush her teeth. Easing back into the bedroom she stepped into a slinky red bathing suit, pulled the length of her hair back into a ponytail and sat down to do her makeup. Minutes later she found Kendrick out on the patio, in deep conversation with Liam. The butler stiffened ever so slightly as she slid the glass doors open and stepped outside, his demeanor suddenly reserved.

Kendrick shifted his gaze in her direction. His breath caught in his chest as he struggled not to react. She was stunning, the scant red fabric complementing every dip and curve. He tried to appear nonchalant, fighting to maintain a poker face. Tossing her an easy smile he crossed one leg over the other as she approached the table, fullness suddenly pressing at the front of his shorts. "Good morning," he said, his voice cracking ever so slightly.

Vanessa smiled brightly. "Good morning. Why didn't you wake me?"

"You looked comfortable," he answered.

"Good morning, Liam."

"Good morning, madam. What might I get for you this morning?"

Vanessa sat down in the chair Liam had pulled out for her. "I'm famished."

"You missed dinner last night. I got to eat the cheesecake all by my lonesome," Kendrick teased.

Vanessa giggled. "I just bet you did," she said, sarcasm tinging her words. She turned her attention back to Liam. "I'd really like pancakes and bacon. Lots of bacon!" she said.

Kendrick cringed. "A heart attack on a plate!" he said teasingly.

Vanessa rolled her eyes. "I can do the health food thing when the honeymoon is over, thank you very much!"

"Coming right up, madam," Liam said as he made his exit.

"I don't like him," Vanessa said, her voice dropping to a whisper when Liam was out of sight.

Kendrick took a sip of his morning beverage, the bright green juice shimmering in the glass. "Why? He seems like a nice guy."

"He reminds me of the guys Marcus used to have around all the time. They all looked sneaky and every one of them had a gun under his jacket."

Kendrick shook his head. "I haven't seen any gun."

"He just looks shady. Maybe you should have your agency run a check on him just to be safe."

Kendrick tried not to laugh aloud, a smirk pulling at his mouth. "I'll do that," he said. He changed the subject. "What would you like to do today?"

"Absolutely nothing. I'm still sore from yesterday."

"You're the one who wanted to be entertained."

"Well, today I just want to lounge around and not do one darn thing."

"Sounds like a plan to me."

There was a brief lull in their conversation as Liam suddenly reappeared with Vanessa's breakfast. The bacon was crisp and the pancakes were light and fluffy, served with freshly whipped butter and warm maple syrup. The food brought a smile back to her face as she dived in with her knife and fork.

Kendrick couldn't keep a straight face as he watched

her eat. She was thoroughly enjoying her meal, consuming it with gusto. It was on the tip of his tongue to
comment but he didn't. She suddenly lifted her eyes to
his and his smile widened, a low chuckle easing past
his lips. She rolled her eyes as she swallowed a forkful of pancake.

"I can't believe you're laughing at me," she said as
she swiped a cloth napkin across her mouth.

"I'm not laughing at you."

"Yes, you are. You're making fun of the fact I have
a healthy appetite."

"I'm not. I'm just trying to figure out where such a
tiny woman can put all that food."

"I have a high metabolism."

"Which is going to slow down in about ten years
and then you're going to get that middle-aged spread."

"I'm sure if that happens I'll spread in all the right
places and still look good," she said as she took another
bite. "I imagine your spread will be beer-gut wide and
not one bit pretty."

"I'll take that bet," Kendrick said.

She shook her head. "You still owe me from the
last bet."

"You haven't told me what you want yet. You were
supposed to tell me last night at dinner."

Vanessa shrugged, a wry smile pulling at her lips.
"I'm still thinking about it."

"That sounds like I should be scared."

"Maybe."

Kendrick chuckled again. He shifted in his seat as
she finished the last bites of her meal. A comfortable

silence wafted between them, only the lull of the ocean sounding through the air. The temperatures were slowly rising and the bright blue sky indicated that it was going to be another beautiful day. He suddenly found himself wishing for rain and a day or two of cold. Anything that might put more clothes on the woman. The moment she'd stepped out the door his body had reacted, desire raging with a vengeance. Every muscle in his body had hardened and he knew that if he stood up anytime soon it would be extremely embarrassing.

She interrupted his thoughts. "Why do you look so uncomfortable?"

He shrugged. "Do I?"

"You look like you could use a good meal. Maybe you should order some bacon," she said.

He shook his head. "I don't think bacon will help my problem."

"So what's wrong with you?"

"Nothing."

She stared at him, her gaze sweeping over his face for a hint of understanding.

He met her stare and shrugged his broad shoulders. "It really isn't anything you need to be concerned with," he said finally.

"Whatever," she said as she pursed her lips tightly together.

Kendrick shifted the conversation. "I need to ask you some questions," he said, refocusing his attention. "I need to know more about your boyfriend, Marcus."

She bristled. "Marcus wasn't my boyfriend."

"But you were in a relationship?"

She shook her head. "It's not what you're thinking. I didn't know him that well. We had only met the week before."

"And you were sleeping with him?"

Her jaw tightened. "I *never* slept with him. We weren't even close to being lovers."

Kendrick's eyes flitted over her face. Her cheeks were flushed and a hint of anger registered in her eyes. His head bobbed. "What do you know about his business with Pedro Fierro?"

She shook her head. "Nothing. That was the first time I'd ever seen the man. Marcus said they had some business to discuss and he told me to walk away. I did. The next thing I knew all hell broke loose. That man was dead and so were my best friends. I don't know why you people keep insisting I know more than I do."

"I have it on good authority that he seems to think you know more than you do."

"Well, he and your good authority are both wrong," she snapped.

He nodded. "I really need you to tell me everything you can, Vanessa. I need you to trust me. Please."

Sincerity seeped past his dark lashes. Vanessa nodded her head slowly as she took a deep breath and told Kendrick about her visit to Miami, starting with why she'd left New York in the first place. When every secret had been spilled, all of her hurts exposed for him to see, she lifted her eyes back to his, her bottom lip quivering.

There was a moment of silence, a hint of tension wafting between them. Tears suddenly fell from beneath her lids and she quickly swiped at her eyes with her hands.

"Please, don't," Kendrick said, shifting forward in his seat. "I didn't mean to make you cry."

"All I want is for this to be over so that I can have my life back. I just want things to be normal again."

Kendrick reached for her hands, clasping them both between his own. "I just needed to make sure you had told me everything you could. I'm sorry if I upset you," he said.

Vanessa's tears continued to fall. "Don't worry about it," she said. "It's fine."

He stared at her, as if unable to find the words to take away the pain in her eyes. He reached a hand out and brushed his fingers against her tears. "I really am sorry, Vanessa. But it's my job to know everything I can."

She suddenly bristled, jumping too quickly to her feet. Her glass of orange juice fell against the table, spilling to the tiled pavers beneath their feet. "Well," she snapped, "I don't have anything else I can tell you. Consider your *job* done well."

Kendrick watched as she stomped off in a huff, disappearing down the sandy trail toward the larger pools on the other side. He tossed a quick look to Liam, who'd appeared out of nowhere, pointing after the woman.

"I'm on it, boss," his associate said with a soft chuckle. "And I thought you had a way with women," he added jokingly.

So did I, Kendrick thought as he tossed up his hands. *So did I.*

* * *

She was angry and even as she fought back her tears all she wanted to do was rage. *His job.* She was nothing more than his job. She took a deep breath to calm her nerves. Dropping down onto one of the lounge chairs by the large pools she pulled her knees to her chest, wrapping her arms around her legs. She didn't have any reason to be angry and she knew it. She knew that Kendrick wasn't there because they were a couple on holiday. He wasn't there because he cared about her and she cared about him. There was only one reason he was there and it had everything to do with his J-O-B.

Kendrick was there to guard her. To keep her safe until she could be the perfect witness. Whether she wanted to be or not. She was his assignment, not his girlfriend. His chore, not his wife. She was even beginning to think that they weren't even friends and she had truly believed there was friendship blooming between them. She swiped at the tears that still misted her eyes.

And then she was angry all over again. He'd been nice to her and she'd believed he liked her. She had let down her guard and had told him about Jarrod and the disaster that had been their relationship. She had revealed her deepest hurt and had allowed herself to be vulnerable just for him to remind her that he was on duty and nothing more.

"Excuse me, madam," a familiar voice said, interrupting her thoughts.

She threw a quick glance over her shoulder. "What do you want, Liam?"

"I was just checking that you were okay. I wanted

to make sure you weren't cut on the broken glass back on the patio."

She shook her head. "I'm fine, thank you."

"Is there anything I can get for you, madam?"

"No. I just want to be left alone, please."

"Yes, madam."

Vanessa tossed one more look over her shoulder to see him as Liam moved back toward the bungalow she was sharing with Kendrick. There was definitely something about that man that made her uncomfortable. But clearly it wasn't Kendrick's *job* to figure out why.

Chapter 8

It was Thanksgiving Day. Vanessa had barely spoken two words to him since blowing up days earlier. She'd taken all of her meals in her room, locking him out. As he'd returned to the bungalow from his run she'd been headed to the pool, brushing past him without saying a thing. She'd spoken to Liam more than him and Kendrick had just about had enough. He had never known any woman to hold a grudge for so long. Take that back. *His sisters could hold a grudge for that long,* Kendrick thought to himself.

He shook his head at the absurdity. But it was Thanksgiving Day and they were not going to spend the holiday at odds with each other. He knocked on the bedroom door. "Vanessa, open up!" When there was no response he knocked a second time. "Open the door, Vanessa, or I'm going to take it off the hinges."

Seconds later he heard her moving on the other side as she stomped across the floor. She swung the door open, eyeing him warily. "What do you want?"

"Get dressed. We're eating in the dining room tonight," he said.

Her gaze narrowed. "I'm not eating anywhere with you, Agent Boudreaux," she snapped as she moved to close the door in his face.

She took a quick step back as Kendrick pushed the door open with a wide palm. He took two steps and was standing directly in front of her, his index finger waving in her face. His tone was low and even with just the slightest hint of attitude. "Get dressed and be ready in the next hour. If you're not ready I'm going to dress you myself and that might not be so pretty."

"You can't..."

"I can," Kendrick said, cutting her words off. "And if you push me, I will." He turned abruptly and moved out of the room.

Vanessa exhaled a deep sigh as she c   door. Her heart was beating heavily a   dampened her palms. Staying mad at him   be a challenge, she thought. The sexy man   down her resolve and he didn't even know it.

Exactly one hour later there was another knock on her bedroom door. This time she pulled it open without him having to call her name.

Vanessa Harrison was stunning as she stood before him, dressed in a little black dress that stopped just above her knee. The sheath was formfitting and complemented her figure. She stood on five-inch stilettos that made her legs look miles long. Her makeup was impeccable and her lush, black hair was loose, flowing over her shoulders. She took his breath away.

"What are you staring at?" Vanessa asked.

"You," he responded, his voice dropping an octave. "You're beautiful."

A slow smile pulled at her mouth. "Thank you," she said, her tone shifting.

He nodded, taking a deep breath. "I hope you're hungry. Liam says they've prepared an incredible Thanksgiving meal."

Vanessa's eyes widened. "It's Thanksgiving already?"

"Yeah. I forgot, too, until Liam reminded me earlier."

She followed behind him as he moved into the living room. He lifted his suit jacket from the back of a cushion, sliding one arm and then the other into it. As he adjusted the lapels, Vanessa eyed him from head to toe. He looked good. Really good. The suit was black, its contemporary lines crisp and stylish. A white dress shirt beneath it that fit his large body to perfection.

Their gazes met and held. Kendrick smiled and once again the warmth of it lifted her heart. She nodded and smiled back.

"Finally," Kendrick said teasingly. "I was really

scared that you were going to scowl through the whole meal."

She rolled her eyes, her smile widening. "I'm still mad at you."

"Why? What did I do?"

"It's not what you did, it's something you said. But it's not important. It doesn't really matter anymore."

He nodded. "It matters to me. So what was it that I said that upset you so much?"

She sighed. "It was that comment about this just being your job. I allowed myself to be vulnerable and opened up to you because I thought we were becoming friends. But I get it. When this is all over you'll go your way and I'll go mine. I understand that this is nothing more than an assignment for you."

He eased his way slowly to where she stood, coming to a stop directly in front of her. "I never meant to hurt your feelings," he said. "But the fact remains I am doing my job whether we like it or not. I have a responsibility to ensure your safety and I don't take that lightly. So first and foremost, I have to be about my business and nothing else."

Vanessa held her breath, suddenly unnerved by the nearness of him. Her knees were quivering, the look he was giving her consuming. She suddenly felt as if she might combust from the intensity of it. She dropped her gaze to the floor, fighting not to lose herself in the look he was giving her.

Kendrick cupped his fingers beneath her chin and lifted her face back to his. He studied her intently before he spoke again. "I don't handle it well when people

I care about shut me out. And I do care about you or I would have had them put someone else on your detail after you were so difficult that first day. So don't do that again," he said, shaking his head. "If we are friends then respect me enough to tell me when you're angry with me so we can talk it out and move past it. I will show you the same courtesy."

Vanessa wasn't used to any man scolding her. Only her father had ever spoken to her that way. It was on the tip of her tongue to balk but she didn't, instead nodding her head in agreement.

Kendrick continued. "And if you haven't figured it out yet, I do like you. I like you a lot. I told you about my most embarrassing moments and if I didn't like you, that would never have happened. Besides…" he said as he reached for her hand. He tangled his fingers between hers, his touch like fuel on a flame. Vanessa gasped loudly, her whole body quivering like jelly. He leaned to press his cheek to hers, warm breath blowing softly against her earlobe. "I get a hard-on every time I'm near you."

Vanessa suddenly laughed, the gesture coming from deep in her midsection. Tears misted her eyes as her laugh became deeper. "I can't believe you said that," she said, cutting her eyes at him.

Kendrick shrugged. "If I offended you I apologize but it's the truth. You excite me. With our situation being so unique I just couldn't say so."

"And you're saying so now?"

"You not talking to me was a real downer, girl. I actually missed you."

She smiled, having felt the exact same way. A moment of quiet passed between them as they both reflected on what was happening between them.

Kendrick took a deep breath. "Let's go get some dinner," he finally said.

In the resort's formal dining room they were shown to an intimate table for two. The crowd was small, with only three other couples. The room's decor was an extraordinary palette of warm greens, winter white and rustic bouquets of orange-toned flowers. The table was adorned with the finest china, gold-colored tableware and cut crystal. The space felt seasonal and fitting for the holiday.

Kendrick pulled out the cushioned chair for Vanessa to take a seat, then moved to the chair opposite her. A waiter suddenly appeared to take their drink order.

"I'd like a glass of merlot," Vanessa said.

Kendrick nodded. "I'll have the same. Thank you."

She gave him a curious look as the waiter moved back toward the bar. "You're actually having wine tonight?"

"One glass. It's a holiday."

She nodded easily as her eyes roamed around the room, taking in her surroundings. "It's so pretty!"

"It is. Almost as pretty as you are."

She smiled. "I think I owe you an apology," she said softly.

Kendrick eyed her questioningly. "For what?"

"For my bad behavior. I don't know why I got so upset with you."

He chuckled. "Because you like me. That's why."

"I do like you and I really like our friendship."

"But you want to be more than friends."

Her face flushed a brilliant shade of red. She rolled her eyes, a smirk pulling at her mouth. "You're a little full of yourself, aren't you?"

Kendrick leaned forward in his seat, resting his elbows against the tabletop. He dropped his chin against his folded hands. "Am I wrong?"

She skirted her gaze from his, the intensity of his stare distracting. When she didn't respond he persisted.

"Answer me. Am I wrong? Are you only interested in our being friends?"

She shrugged. "I admit it. I've thought about more."

Kendrick still stared at her intently. "How much more?"

She finally locked gazes with the man, her own eyes narrowing seductively. "I've fantasized about us being together. It's hard not to when you're wearing nothing but Speedos all day long."

Kendrick laughed. "I have never worn a pair of Speedos."

"They might as well be. Tonight's the first time you've actually had clothes on since we got here."

"The bikini queen is complaining about my wardrobe," he said flippantly. He leaned back in his seat, amusement in his eyes.

Before she could comment the waiter and two other staff members came bearing their evening meal. Kendrick tossed her a bright smile as they were being served. The traditional meal was decadent and lavish: classic roast turkey, stuffing, cranberry sauce, sautéed green beans, garlic mashed potatoes and gravy, honey-glazed carrots, yeast rolls and warm pumpkin pie for dessert. It was more than Vanessa had imagined. Her eyes were wide as she took it all in. "Wow!" she exclaimed.

Kendrick nodded in agreement. He rested both elbows on the table and extended his flattened palms toward her. "Let's say grace," he said, meeting her gaze evenly.

Vanessa dropped her palms against his, heat tingling through her body as he took hold of her hands and bowed his head in prayer.

"Heavenly Father, bless this food we're about to receive for the nourishment of our bodies. In your son's name we pray. Amen." He gave her hands a quick squeeze before letting them go.

"Amen," Vanessa echoed softly. She clenched her fists together to stall the quiver of electricity racing through her limbs. She reached for the platters and began to serve both their plates. Kendrick sat back and watched her.

For the next few minutes neither spoke, enjoying the meal. The food was good and as they began to eat, she realized just how famished they both were. When dessert was finally served Kendrick ordered two cups of coffee.

"This was wonderful," Vanessa intoned. "I love good food."

"I can tell," he said as he reached across the table, his cloth napkin in hand. He swiped at the side of her face, removing a stripe of whipped cream from her cheek.

Vanessa laughed. "I like to see you happy," Kendrick said. "You're not that cute when you're mad. In fact, you're downright ugly when you make that 'I hate the world' face."

"Thank you. You have such a way with words," she teased.

"You can always trust me to tell you the truth."

"Really?"

"All day long."

She tossed a quick look over her shoulder, her voice dropping to a low whisper. She shifted forward, the gesture almost conspiratorial. "So, do you really get an erection every time you're near me?"

He leaned forward in his seat, meeting her across the table. His head nodded up and down as a wide grin spread across his face. "No," he said out loud.

Vanessa laughed. "Liar!"

Vanessa changed out of her clothes, hanging her little black dress back in her closet. The temperatures outside were still excessively warm, feeling more like the dead of summer than late fall. She found herself wishing for a winter chill and the smell of snow. A northeastern cold front always made the holiday feel like a holiday. She slipped into a tank top and a pair of shorts.

As she eased her way outside through the sliding glass doors, she saw Kendrick sitting on the edge of the infinity pool, his long legs in the water. They both grinned, excitement wafting through the late-night air.

"I just had a quick swim. It felt really good," he said

as she joined him. "I'm so glad you're here with me tonight."

She took a seat beside him, kicking her legs through the water. "Thank you," she said softly.

"What did I do?"

"You made it a great day and I really appreciate that."

He nodded as he reached for her hand and held it. Vanessa leaned her head against his shoulder, staring out to the quarter moon in the dark sky. They sat quietly together for some time, neither saying a word.

Kendrick turned at the sound of soft footsteps. Liam was rounding the corner.

"Good evening, sir. Good evening, madam. I just wanted to check to see if you needed anything before I retired for the evening."

Kendrick gave Vanessa a quick look. She shook her head no. "We're good, Liam. I appreciate you asking."

"Yes, sir. Well, you both have a good evening," he said as he withdrew quietly.

Vanessa shook her head. "I'm telling you, there's something not right about that man."

Kendrick laughed. "Well, I had him checked out for you and his record came back clear."

"You're sure?"

He nodded. "Positive. He's a nice Irish boy from Northern Ireland. Studied to be a teacher, did a short stint in the National Theater in England, then worked the cruise lines for a few years. He's twice divorced, has two sons and dates a Swedish model named Vega. Pleasure Island hired him a few years ago. He came highly recommended and has had glowing reviews since."

"I can't believe you actually checked."

"You were concerned and it's my *job* to make sure you're comfortable," he said, emphasizing the word *job*.

Nodding, Vanessa leaned in closer to his side and Kendrick wrapped an arm around her shoulders. As they sat in the quiet he leaned to press a gentle kiss against her forehead, as if it was the easiest, most natural thing he'd done in a very long time. He kissed her a second time as he pulled her closer against him.

Vanessa suddenly kicked her legs in the water, splashing them both. "Let's go!" she exclaimed, moving onto her feet.

Kendrick looked up at her. "Where?"

"You still owe me and I'm ready to collect."

He laughed. "You still haven't told me what you're claiming."

"I guess you need to get up and come on, then," she said, her hands falling against her thin waist.

He shook his head. "Now I'm scared," he said as he lifted his legs out of the pool of water and stood up. As he came to his feet Vanessa took his hand and pulled him along behind her.

She led the way down the stone path toward the beach. The sky above was blue black, just the shimmer of moon and twinkling of stars lighting the ground around them. When they reached the edge of the water she turned toward him, a wide grin across her face.

Kendrick eyed her curiously. "What are you up to?" he questioned.

"We're going skinny-dipping," she said matter-of-factly.

Kendrick hesitated for a brief moment, his eyes widened in disbelief. He cocked his head as he stared at her. "I don't think that's a good idea, Ms. Harrison."

She laughed. "Get your clothes off, chicken. You bet, you lost, I won, and I'm collecting."

His head was waving from side to side. "We need to talk about this."

"Anything I want. Isn't that what you said?"

He laughed. "I did say that."

"Then drop 'em," she said, pointing to his shorts.

She reached for the hem of her tank top and proceeded to pull the garment up and over her head. She was braless, her pert breasts standing at full attention. Her nipples were hardened orbs, reminding him of dark molasses candy. Her stomach rippled, reflecting some serious work in the gym. She looped her thumbs in the waistband of her shorts and pushed them down to her ankles. Stepping out of them, she kicked the garment and her lace thong up the sandy beach. Her smile was miles wide as she took two steps back, her hands on her hips.

Kendrick gasped, a low breath blowing past his lips. His own grin spread wide and full across his face. He took a deep breath as he slowly pushed his own shorts down over his hips. A full erection protruded in her direction as if she were a snake charmer who'd beguiled the serpent right out of his pants.

Vanessa's grin widened and then she turned, racing out to the ocean as she threw her body beneath the watery blanket. Right on her heels Kendrick raced after her, plunging his own body into the warm waters behind her.

Laughter rang loudly through the late-night air as the two frolicked from one end of the beach to the other. There was a moment when Vanessa went quiet, lost somewhere in the darkness, and just when Kendrick was ready to panic she popped up behind him, her hands encircling his waist, her laughter like warm honey to his ears. He spun her around into his arms and held her tightly, pulling her to his chest. Her legs wrapped around his waist and she locked her ankles against the curve of his buttocks. They were both breathing heavily, gasping for air.

Vanessa pressed her cheek to his, savoring the warmth of his skin as she wrapped her slender arms around his neck. One of his hands danced along her spine, the other cupped beneath her buttocks, holding her up. He felt good against her, strong and solid, and if she could have she would have stayed there forever.

Kendrick's heart was beating heavily in his chest. The heavy rhythm was like the deep bass in the middle of a jazz syncopation. His pulse was quick and heat flushed every muscle in his body. He slid his large hand across her back and up to her neck, his fingers gently massaging her skin. He snaked his fingers into the strands of her hair and pulled gently, her head falling back against her shoulders. She gasped as he pressed his mouth to that spot beneath her chin, biting at the soft flesh. Vanessa purred ever so softly, the lilt of her voice causing him to harden even more. He trailed a line of damp kisses over her chin and along the profile of her jaw. He pulled back, his stare meeting hers. Her lips were parted and she bit down against her bottom lip. He drew his palm beneath her chin, his thumb dancing at the edge of her mouth as rivulets of water dripped over her cheeks. Anticipation danced in her eyes and he could feel her holding her breath, the air catching somewhere deep in her chest. With nothing but desire raging between them Kendrick plunged his mouth against hers, capturing her lips with his own.

The kiss was like nothing she had ever known before. Vanessa felt her entire body quiver with excitement, every nerve ending exploding with sheer pleasure. She inhaled him, his cologne holding hands with the scent of sea air. She could feel her heart beating and her feminine spirit was suddenly throbbing with a vengeance.

Kendrick's lips danced over hers, skin sliding like silk against silk. She tasted sweet like the dessert they'd shared, the hint of red wine on her breath. He suddenly couldn't imagine himself kissing any other woman ever again. The realization knocked him offside and he felt himself gasp. He tightened the hold he had on her, her pelvis heated and damp against his lower abdomen. His manhood twitched and pulsed with a vengeance.

Kendrick eased his tongue past her lips and Vanessa allowed him in, her own tasting him eagerly. Time suddenly came to a standstill and then a wave of water crashed into them, knocking Kendrick off his feet. Sliding beneath the swell they clung to each other, neither breaking the hold. When the waters came to a rest he pulled them back up, swept her into his arms and carried her back to the beach. When he reached the white sands he put her back on her feet. They stood together for some time, completely lost in each other as they traded easy caresses.

Kissing her one last time Kendrick pulled himself from her. He shook his head, his eyes closed as he found himself lost in thought. He took a deep breath and then another as Vanessa fought to calm her own breathing. Opening his eyes he met her gaze and held it, something shimmering in her dark orbs that he didn't recognize. He leaned to kiss her cheek.

"We can't do this," he whispered as he rested his face against hers. "And I want to, Vanessa. God knows I do, but we just can't."

Vanessa quivered in his arms.

"I have a responsibility…" he started.

She pressed her fingers to his lips, stalling his words. She nodded her head. Before he could say another word she pressed her hands to his chest and reached up on her tippy toes to lightly kiss his mouth one last time. She whispered a soft good-night as tears rained down over her cheeks. Turning away from him she sprinted toward the bungalow, disappearing inside.

Hours later Kendrick was still sitting, Buddha-like, naked under the moonlight. Every thought in his mind was about Vanessa and him and the entanglement between them. For the first time in his life he was conflicted, his personal life clashing with his career. And despite the anguish holding him hostage, he was thankful as the notion of him and her together danced in his head and his heart.

Chapter 9

For the first day since their arrival there was no sun. The sky was gray, clouds covering the deep blue sky they'd both grown accustomed to. No one needed to tell either of them that there was a storm coming. You could feel it in the temperatures that had fallen and the smell in the early-morning air that was rich and earthy. The resort was making preparations for the possibility of a hurricane, as the winds churned somewhere in the distance. The weather pattern had changed considerably.

When Vanessa made her way into the living area Kendrick was in deep discussion with Liam, the two men huddled together in a corner of the room.

"Many of the guests are flying out this morning, sir. However, if you choose to stay we will do everything in our power to ensure your safety."

Kendrick nodded. "The weather reports are predicting it's going to bypass the island. We may get some residual winds and rain but I don't think it's going to be anything I need to be concerned about. We'll be staying."

"Certainly, sir," the butler responded. "I'll inform the front desk. We do ask that you both remain inside until the bad weather has passed. The winds are picking up and we don't want to take any unnecessary risks."

Both men tossed her a look. Kendrick smiled.

"Good morning, madam!" Liam crooned, his voice lifting eagerly. "What might I get for you this morning?"

She gave them both a warm smile back. "Yogurt and granola would be good this morning," she said cheerily. "And bacon. Have to have my bacon!"

Liam nodded. "Right away, madam."

As the man left to fetch her morning meal, Kendrick stood staring at her. She stood nervously, her gaze flitting everywhere but on him.

"Are you mad at me?" he questioned, his tone warm and endearing.

She shook her head. "Not at all. Actually I have great respect for your self-control."

Kendrick chuckled. "Me, too! Telling you no was the hardest thing I have ever had to do."

She laughed with him. "It was a new experience for me, too!"

She moved to the dining table and Kendrick joined her. As she reached his side she eased an arm around his waist and hugged him. Kendrick kissed the top of her head and then dropped his mouth against hers. The kiss was sweet and gentle and easy and though he seemed to enjoy lingering in it, he moved away instead, reaching to pull out a chair for her.

"Did you sleep well?" he asked as he took his own seat.

"No. I kept thinking about you."

He nodded. "I didn't sleep well, either."

Their gazes locked as they sat in reflection, thinking about the hours since they'd parted last night. Vanessa had tossed and turned until the wee hours of the morning. More times than she cared to count she had thought about going back to him. She'd obsessed over his touch, the kisses they'd shared, the nearness of him, her body wrapped like a blanket around his. She'd fantasized about him coming to her, pushing his way into the bedroom to take her. Wanting him to possess her body and soul. It had taken every ounce of her fortitude not to give in to the temptation.

Kendrick appeared lost in his thoughts, too. They blew deep sighs at the same time and then laughed at the hilarity of their situation.

"I imagine you have women chasing after you with every assignment," she said.

He shook his head. "Not at all. It's very rare that my assignment is to keep my eyes on a beautiful woman."

"So tell me about your past relationships?" she asked. "How did they work with your job?"

Kendrick shrugged. "There really isn't anything to tell. I've dated but I can count on one hand the women I've dated more than once. And I'd still have fingers left

over! I told you, this job is not conducive to a relationship. It's hard enough just trying to keep up with my
family because I'm gone more than I'm home."

Vanessa paused as Liam appeared with their breakfast. When they were served he made his exit just as
quickly. She took a sip of her orange juice before she
spoke again. "Moving to New York was really the first
time I've been away from my family and even then my
mother was never too far away. I could always call her
whenever and she flew in monthly to go shopping, so
we had a standing lunch date. This is the first time I've
ever been away so long and not been able to call. I can't
imagine being away for months and not being able to
at least talk to them. I don't know how you do that."

He suddenly stood up, moving out of the room. Vanessa called after him, confusion washing over her expression. "Kendrick? Is everything okay? Kendrick?"

She was just about to go after him when he returned,
a cell phone in his palm. Moving back to her side he
handed the device to her.

"Call your mother. Talk as long as you want, but
please be mindful. Don't say anything about where we
are. That's for her safety as well as yours."

Vanessa's eyes were wide. "Really?"

He gently pressed his palm to the side of her face as
he nodded his head.

Reaching her arms around him Vanessa hugged him
tightly, giving him a quick peck on the lips. She dropped
back into her seat and dialed. When her mother answered, tears misted her eyes.

"Hi, Mom!" she exclaimed excitedly.

* * *

Kendrick kissed the top of her head then moved out of her space, allowing her some privacy. He trusted that she would heed his warning. He also had his own telephone call to make.

Stepping out onto the patio he pulled a second phone from his pocket and dialed. The wind was definitely picking up but the temperature was still fairly comfortable. He was slightly surprised when his sister Maitlyn answered the call.

"Hello?"

"Hey, Mattie!"

"Hey, yourself. What's going on?"

"I just needed to chat with your husband for a minute."

"Is something wrong with Vanessa?"

"Maitlyn, really?"

"What? I was just concerned."

"Well, she's doing fine."

"And you're good?"

"Yeah…everything is going really well. Now, may I please speak with Zak?"

"No."

Kendrick bristled ever so slightly. "No?"

"I said no. My husband is tied up at the moment so if this isn't an emergency you can't talk to him."

"You're joking, right?"

"I am serious as a heart attack."

Kendrick sighed. "I really need to speak with him, Maitlyn. It's important. I…I need…" He paused.

"You need advice," she said, the comment more of a statement than a question.

"Yes."

"So, what's your problem?"

Kendrick tossed a quick glance back through the glass doors. There was a bright smile on Vanessa's face and she was deep in conversation, her entire body animated. She looked happy and the joy shining on her face made him smile. In all honesty he hated that there was so much distance between him and his family. When he did see his siblings it was always about trying to catch up and more times than not he felt out of the loop. Despite the love they shared there was a level of disconnect that he couldn't deny and much of it was from his own making. Asking Maitlyn to research property for him had everything to do with him wanting things to change. His growing feelings for Vanessa had him owning that for the very first time.

He turned back to his current conversation.

"Did Zak ever have any reservations about being with you when you two were on the cruise ship?"

"No, never."

"Not even a little? I mean, he was on assignment. Didn't he ever think about that?"

"No, because I wasn't his assignment. When we spent time together it was always about our attraction to each other and nothing else."

Kendrick blew a heavy breath past his lips. He stared off to the rising waters on the shoreline. His sister's voice rang in his ear.

"You can't spend the rest of your life on the front line

fighting bad guys, Kendrick. You're going to be too old for this at some point. Don't you want to retire shooting hoops with your grandchildren instead of being all alone with bad people still shooting at you?"

Kendrick chuckled ever so softly. "Are you sure I can't speak with Zak?"

"Positive. Go spend some time with Vanessa. Get to know her. Romance her a little. Zak will call you later."

"I really hate it when you take control, Maitlyn. You know that, right?"

His sister laughed. "Zak loves it!" she said as she disconnected the line.

Kendrick was still laughing when he moved back inside. Vanessa had already disconnected her own call. She jumped to her feet and rushed to his side, her face still aglow, the joy shimmering in her eyes.

"Thank you! Thank you so much!" she exclaimed as she threw her arms around his neck.

Kendrick wrapped his own arms around her waist, lifting her off her feet. He held her tightly, suddenly not wanting to let go. He wanted to kiss her but he knew that if he did he wouldn't be able to stop.

"So everything is good at home?" he questioned, finally letting her go.

"Yes. And I didn't tell them where I was or anything," she reassured him.

Kendrick smiled. "I know you didn't."

"They still haven't found Gabrielle's grandparents, though. Apparently they moved but no one knows where. My father says my brother Juan is personally searching for them. I got to speak with Gabi and she told me she's going to the mall to see Santa Claus. It was so cute! My mother says she's a handful but they're enjoying having her around. She says she's getting a taste of what it will be like to have grandchildren."

Kendrick smiled. "That's good."

Vanessa tipped up on her toes and pressed her lips to his cheek. "Thank you again," she said softly.

He nodded, his eyes locked on her face. As she stepped in closer to him, her body brushing warmly against his, her joy was infectious. He laughed heartily and then without giving it a second thought, he kissed her.

Chapter 10

The rains had finally come, as did heavy gales of wind. The resort's staff had secured all the patio furniture and drawn the storm shutters on the windows and doors. Kendrick and Vanessa were locked in, safe and secure from the inclement weather.

Music played on the bungalow's Bose system, low jazz tones billowing through the late-afternoon air. The two had been laughing and joking for most of the day, their conversations easy and casual.

Kendrick sat at one end of the sofa, his legs outstretched. Vanessa sat at the other end, her legs extended over his. She was sipping on a mug of hot tea while he drank coconut water. Time seemed to fly and they learned more and more about each other.

"Why do you hate to exercise?" Kendrick questioned. "I mean, with your abs I'd think you loved it."

"It loves my body and I work hard, but I have to. I'm not naturally thin and I come from a family who has suffered with diabetes, high blood pressure and heart disease. I know I have to take care of myself if I want to stay healthy. Besides, I like to eat. And to eat the foods I love means I have to stay in the gym whether I like it or not."

"You do like to eat!" Kendrick teased. "You get excited just talking about food!"

Vanessa laughed, fanning her hand in his direction. "I am not that bad."

"Say something about bacon," Kendrick commanded.

"Bacon? It's really good when it's crispy. You can eat it on a salad. Bacon is…"

"See!" Kendrick exclaimed. "Got you twitching you want some so bad!"

Vanessa laughed again. "You are so not funny."

"But you're laughing."

"I'm laughing because you're such a fool."

A sudden gust of wind blew harshly and glass shattered in the distance. Kendrick pushed her legs off his and rose from his seat. He moved to the sliding glass doors and peeked out. A large tree limb had slammed into one of the glass tabletops propped against the wall, shattering it. Once he confirmed that it was only bad weather posing a threat to them, he moved back to his seat. Sitting back down, he pulled Vanessa's legs onto his lap again, and gently massaged her feet. His touch was warm and teasing and as he palmed the bottoms of her toes, she smiled.

Vanessa slid into the sensations that were teasing her nerve endings. His hands felt good and she found herself wishing he would never stop. "You're very good at that," she said.

Kendrick nodded. "I'm very good at everything I do."

Vanessa rolled her eyes. "I'm sure there's something you're not good at."

"Well, when you figure out what that is, let me know," he said. There was a smug smirk on his face. "So what are you good at?" he asked.

"I'm a fantastic baker. My double chocolate fudge cupcakes will make you slap yo' mama they're so good. Oh, and I make the best cheesecake in the whole wide world."

"I'll have to taste it to believe it," he said.

She fanned her hand at him. "You'll be smacking your lips, your hips, and slapping yo' mama. And I like your mother. I'm going to feel bad for you when she slaps you back!"

He laughed heartily. "What else?"

Vanessa paused for a brief moment as she reflected on his question. "I'm a darn good filmmaker," she said finally.

"That's what you're in school for, right?"

She nodded. "I only have one more semester till graduation but I've been making mini movies since I knew what a camera was. In fact, this is the longest time I've ever been without my video camera. I'm used to taking it everywhere."

Kendrick eased slightly forward in his seat. He still caressed her feet. "Where's it at?" he questioned, shifting his gaze to her face.

She shrugged. "Still with my things in Miami. We left in such a hurry that I forgot to grab it."

He nodded slowly. "Were you filming while you were in Miami?"

"Yeah. I took film of Gabi that I was going to make into a mini movie for Alexandra and Paolo for Christmas," she said. She paused as she thought back to the trips she and Gabrielle had taken to the beach and playground, neither having a care in the world. The memories made her melancholy and she shook the sensation, willing herself back to the moment. She shook her head and forced a smile onto her face when she realized Kendrick was studying her.

Kendrick took a deep breath. He hesitated for a moment before asking his next question. "Did you ever do any filming when you were with Marcus Bennett?"

She paused, sensing he'd shifted from Kendrick the friend to Kendrick the secret agent. She exhaled a deep sigh as she nodded her head. "I did. I shot a lot of film when we were on Marcus's yacht. It was always a party, lots of people, and I thought it would make some good footage for something later down the road."

Kendrick had stopped massaging her feet. He was now leaned forward. "Where's that film, Vanessa?"

"All my stuff is digital. It's uploaded to my cloud account."

Kendrick was suddenly anxious. He jumped and Vanessa's eyes widened.

"What?" she questioned.

"I need to see that footage. It might explain why Bennett's got people looking for you."

"He has people looking for me?"

Kendrick met the look she was giving him. Seemingly realizing he had spoken out of turn, the words falling from his mouth before he could catch them. He reached for her hand, clasping her fingers between his palms.

"You're safe. I hope you trust that," he said, his tone calm.

She took a deep breath, nodding her head. The look he gave her was soothing. "I do," she whispered softly. "You make me feel safe."

Hours later it was still raining cats and dogs, the harsh roar of thunder and lightning breaking through the late-night sky. They'd lost power and Liam had arrived with a multitude of candles, two flashlights and a decadent meal of lobster and shrimp salad atop a bed of romaine lettuce. Before bidding them a good-night he lit a fire in both fireplaces, giving them light in both the living room and the bedroom.

The flicker of flames cast a warm glow around the space and with the harsh winds and rain outside, the romantic hideaway felt abundantly comfortable. After playing a horde of board games and a few rounds of Truth or Dare, Kendrick excused himself to go check that all was still well. Disappearing out the front door he was gone just long enough for Vanessa to become concerned. She had risen from her seat to peer out the blinds when he returned, drenched from the onslaught of water falling from the sky.

"You're soaked," Vanessa exclaimed. She hurried to the bathroom, returning seconds later with an oversize beach towel. She stood watching as Kendrick pulled off his T-shirt and then she stepped in to wrap the towel around his broad shoulders.

"Thank you," he said, swiping at the moisture across his face and head.

"Everything okay?"

He nodded. "I just wanted to make sure no one could sneak up on us unexpected."

She shook her head. "I doubt even Marcus would think to come out in this weather."

"You can never be too sure."

A faint smile pulled at her mouth. "You should get out of those wet pants," she said. "Then sit in front of the fireplace. We don't want you to catch cold."

Kendrick grinned. "Are you trying to get me naked?"

Her eyes rolled. "Please, I've already seen you naked."

He laughed. "I know. That's why I asked."

She laughed with him. "I wasn't impressed," she said. She held up her hand, spreading her thumb and index finger an inch or so apart.

"You're one to talk with those lopsided boobs of yours!"

Vanessa's eyes widened, a look of astonishment on her face. "My boobs are not lopsided!" she exclaimed.

"Looks like you got a plum and a lemon stuck in your bikini top!"

She swatted a playful hand at him.

"I'm dead serious," Kendrick said. "Plum and lemon," he said, tweaking one of her breasts and then the other.

Vanessa slapped an arm across her chest, surprise registering on her face. "You've got some nerve!" she said as she lifted her hand to punch him playfully a second time.

Kendrick jumped out of her reach, egging her on. "You're right," he teased. "They're more like a lemon and a grape. A lemon and a grape," he echoed as he made a mad dash to the other side of the couch with Vanessa in hot pursuit.

It became a game of chase as the duo raced around the room like grade-schoolers.

Vanessa laughed heartily, the wealth of it gut-deep. She suddenly came to a quick stop and turned, the gesture unexpected; Kendrick reacted too slowly, running right into her. As they slammed into one another Vanessa accidently kneed Kendrick in the groin. With the wind knocked out of his sails he doubled over in pain, clutching himself between the legs. He dropped to the ground, rolling onto his side as tears misted his eyes.

Vanessa slapped her hand over her mouth, gasping loudly. "Oh, my God…oh, my God…oh, my God!" she repeated over and over. She dropped down to the carpeted floor beside him. "I am so sorry! Are you okay?"

Kendrick was still gasping for air. "You…you broke me," he finally muttered.

Vanessa laughed. "Now you're only a half inch," she said.

Kendrick suddenly grabbed her, flipping her onto the floor beside him. His fingers danced across her midsection as he tickled her until she gasped for air.

"Stop! Stop!" she exclaimed between giggles. "Stop, Kendrick!"

Kendrick rolled his body against hers, pulling her into his arms. He held her close as they both panted heavily. He lifted himself ever so slightly, his gaze connecting to hers.

Vanessa's breath caught deep in her chest as she met the intense look he was giving her. His stare was searing, piercing her soul deeply. There was something in his eyes that pulled at all of her emotions. Saline burned hot behind her lids but they were tears of joy and happiness. She pressed her hand to his chest, her fingers stoking the inferno that would be difficult to cool.

She trailed her fingers across his breastbone down to the taut muscles of his six-pack. His breathing was heavy, his chest rising and falling with anticipation. She drew her hand around his waist until her palm was pressing against his back. Still staring into his eyes she pulled him to her and he went willingly.

Kendrick leaned toward her as if he had no control of his body. As he got closer she closed her eyes, anticipation painting her expression. Closing his own eyes he kissed her. His lips touched hers, grazing them lightly. His heart began to beat faster and his breath quickened. The kiss was easy and gentle, both needing that touch. He kissed her hungrily, allowing his lips to glide over her lips. Heat swelled thick and full between them, the moment combustible.

Vanessa slid her hands around his neck and pulled him in tightly. She kissed him back with all the passion she could muster. Her lips parted as she relished the sensations sweeping through her body. She was breathing him in and her spirit felt nourished, her body completely energized. She heard herself moan, a soft guttural rejoicing that rang through the air.

Kendrick pushed his tongue past the line of her teeth and they parted easily, allowing him inside. He tasted her and she was as sweet as a decadent flavoring of honey and cinnamon. His tongue danced alongside her tongue, an easy two-step that quickly shifted into a rhythmic fox-trot. He slid one hand beneath her waist, his palm resting against the curve of her buttocks. The other slid behind her head, tangling in the length of her hair as he covered her body with his own.

Vanessa's hands skated across his back and she found herself clinging to him. Heat coursed beneath her skin, her muscles quivering intensely. The synapses in her brain were on overload, her body functioning with a mind of its own. The wanting was unbearable. It was the sweetest pain she had ever known.

Kendrick suddenly broke the connection, needing to catch his breath. He pressed his forehead to hers, her skin damp and heated. His mind was racing but the desire in his heart overshadowed the last remnants of doubt floating through his head. He wanted her and in that moment nothing else mattered.

He suddenly pushed himself up onto his knees, star-

ing down at her. Her face was flushed, color tinting
her cheeks. She bit down against her bottom lip as she
lifted her gaze to his. Desire shimmered in her eyes.
Her back was arched, her chest heaving up and down as
she panted softly. Her legs were parted around his, one
bare foot sliding up and down against his calf. Kendrick suddenly trailed a finger against her inner thigh
and she jumped, her eyes widening. A smile pulled at
her mouth.

Kendrick smiled back as he stood. The seductive
bend to his full lips made her gasp out loud. She lifted
her torso, rising up on her elbows to watch him. He
undid his belt first, then slowly unfastened the metal
buttons on his denim jeans. When he pushed them past
his hips and down to the floor beneath his bare feet,
his erection protruded eagerly. He wrapped his hands
around his member and stroked it gently.

Vanessa giggled. "Okay, so maybe it's a little bigger
than this," she said as she gestured with her thumb and
finger. And it was. Her eyes were widening. He was
full and thick and hard as steel.

Kendrick laughed. "Oh, it's much bigger than that,"
he said as he bent down to step out of his pants. He
reached into the back pocket of the garment and pulled
his wallet from inside. Digging through the leather case
he pulled a condom from an inner compartment. He
kicked his jeans behind him and dropped back to his
knees. He leaned forward and slid his hands beneath
the hem of her T-shirt. Vanessa sat upright, crossing
her arms in front of herself as she helped him pull the
garment up and over her head. His eyes dropped to her

breasts. Her nipples were hard protrusions, like dark chocolate kisses against her honeyed complexion. He teased one and then the other with the back of his fingers before lifting his eyes back to hers.

"A grapefruit and a grapefruit," he said, his voice dropping an octave.

Lying back against the carpet Vanessa lifted her buttocks, pushing her shorts and thong off her hips. Kendrick's eyes followed her movements, his gaze moving from her stomach down to the perfectly manicured landing strip between her legs. When she tossed her bottoms aside he looked back to her face.

"Are you sure about this?" he suddenly questioned.

Vanessa nodded her consent. "Are you?"

He nodded with her. Dropping back against her body he kissed her again, his mouth claiming hers eagerly. His hands danced from one end of her torso to the other. His touch was intoxicating and with each stroke and every caress Vanessa felt heady, everything spinning around her. With every pass of his fingers, his mouth followed, his tongue hot and teasing against her skin.

Vanessa pulled the prophylactic into her hand, tearing the wrapper with her teeth. Reaching between them she sheathed his engorged member, stroking him gently as she did. He tensed when she touched him, fighting not to explode from the sensation. Her hand was hot and taunting as she pumped her fist up and down against him.

He dropped his head to her breasts, his tongue lashing at one nipple and then the other. He suckled the hardened nubs between his teeth and he felt her bristle with pleasure as she dropped a hand against the back of his head, pulling him tight to her. He wanted to linger in the moment and savor each sensation sweeping between them.

Vanessa moaned his name over and over again. Her entire body was on sensory overload, every nerve ending firing hot through her system. No man had ever had her begging so wantonly, desperate to be taken. She parted her legs unabashedly, her hand guiding him to the door of her most private place. She pushed her pelvis upward, eager to feel him inside of her.

Kendrick pushed forward, entering her easily. They both gasped loudly, her muffled cry lost in their kisses. She welcomed him in and with one hard thrust he buried himself deeply. The muscles of her inner lining contracted and pulsed as she adjusted to the feel of him. He tightened the hold he had around her torso and Vanessa hugged him closer.

He made sweet love to her, a slow push and pull of his hips. It was teasing at first, then possessive, his body claiming every square inch of hers. He stroked her in and out, in and out, and with each thrust Vanessa met him with her own up-and-down rhythm. His kisses trailed from her mouth to her cheeks, across the line of her profile down to her neck and back. His breathing turned ragged and the moaning became rhythmic as their climax neared.

They were caught up in the moment, their bodies sweaty, moving against each other feverishly. Outside, the rain beat harshly against the thatched roof. Flames crackled in the fireplace and the flickering candles perfumed the air around them. He stroked her faster and faster, their bodies moving beyond control until wave after wave of pleasure hit Vanessa first and then Kendrick, their orgasms coming one after the other. The moment was intense, the eruption volcanic. Vanessa clung to him, her body shaking as his quivered in sync.

The last quivers of their climax left them both panting heavily, sharing the oxygen that billowed between them. The weight of his body rested against her and she savored the feel of him. As his breathing finally eased, his body temperature returning to a semblance of normal, he pressed one more kiss to her cheek then nuzzled his nose into her neck. As the fullness of his manhood subsided, falling from her body, he pulled himself off her.

Vanessa rolled onto her side as he curled his body against the curve of her backside.

Minutes later Vanessa was snoring softly. Wrapping his body around hers, Kendrick wrapped his arm around her waist, his palm pressed to the flat of her abdomen as he drifted off to sleep with her.

Chapter 11

When Vanessa woke Kendrick was gone and she was alone in the large bed. The memory of the night before was still fresh in her memory and she found herself grinning like the Cheshire cat. She stretched her body against the mattress top, kicking the sheets from around her feet.

She pressed her palm between her legs, tightening her thighs and knees together. She was just sore enough, the ache a sweet reminder of their time together. They had made love for hours. Over and over again, christening every corner of their honeymoon suite. The last time had been just before sunrise when they'd finally found their way to the bed. Vanessa couldn't remember anything else being so amazing. Kendrick had made love to her and it felt like actual love. Every caress, every touch, every stroke was filled with emotion, the sensations corporeal. A shiver ran the length of her spine as she thought about it, and him.

Throwing her legs off the bed she moved onto her feet, staring at the landscape outside. The storm had passed, nothing remaining but the debris strewn across the manicured lawn. Leaf-laden limbs protruded from the white sand on the beach. But the ocean water and the early-morning sky were both like blue ice, one shimmering as brightly as the other. As the new-day sun was beginning to rise so was the morning heat.

She moved into the bathroom and entered the shower, turning on the hot water. As she waited for the water to warm she moved to the sink and brushed her teeth. She was just about to step inside the shower when she heard Kendrick come back. He was having a conversation with Liam, both their voices echoing from the front room. When she heard the door close behind the butler she wrapped a towel around her naked body and went to greet Kendrick.

The minute Vanessa laid eyes on Kendrick a warm tingle rushed through her body. He looked so good. Morning shadow gave him the hint of a beard. He was dressed casually in running pants, racing sneakers and a ribbed tank top. The short length of his hair was picked out and his face was flushed from his morning run. When he saw her he smiled. "Good morning."

"Hi. How was your run?" Vanessa asked.

He moved to her side and she caught his scent in the air around her. She took a deep breath and held it.

He leaned to kiss her lips. "It was good. You should go with me sometime."

She chuckled softly. "Thanks, but no thanks. That's the one thing I don't do."

"Maybe one day I can change your mind."

"Let's not bet on that," she said.

Kendrick laughed, shaking his head as he stared at her. Vanessa could barely breathe as she watched him take her in with his eyes, his gaze skating from the top of her head to her manicured toes. They roamed over her body as if he could see right through the towel, taking in all of her hidden treasures. She shivered when he reached out and ran his finger along the top edge of the towel, caressing the round of her cleavage.

When he touched her she closed her eyes and sighed, inhaling him a second time. When she opened her eyes there was nothing but pure desire painting his expression.

"You look like you were just about to get into the shower," he said. The sound of the water running echoed in the background.

She nodded. "I was. Why don't you come join me?" She extended her hand in invitation.

Kendrick took her hand and she pulled him toward the bedroom. She watched him step out of his clothes as they moved down the hallway. And by the time they made it to the shower Vanessa had dropped her towel to the tiled floor.

The water was just hot enough, both of them relaxing beneath the wet spray. There were multiple shower-heads in the tiled enclosure and water rained down from every direction. The wet liquid pulsed, massaging taut muscles as it caressed bare skin.

Kendrick enjoyed watching the wet drops make their way down her body. He reached out to comb his fingers through her wet hair, the luxurious strands clinging to her skin. She passed him a bottle of shampoo and he gently massaged suds from her scalp down to the end of each strand. When her hair was washed, conditioned and rinsed he soaped her body, allowing his hands to glide over her curves. As he dipped his fingers in the juncture between her legs, her nipples grew hard and he felt the initial quiver of an erection lengthen in his southern quadrant.

Vanessa took a deep breath and held it for a quick moment before blowing it past her lips. "If you keep that up," she said, "we're never getting out of this shower."

Kendrick laughed as she turned in his arms, taking the bar of soap from his hands. "I don't know if I want to get out of this shower," he said as she began to reciprocate his touch. He leaned back against the tiles as she drew her hands down the length of his body.

Steam rose through the space, clouding the view. Kendrick pulled her close, nuzzling his body against hers. He held her, enjoying the feel of her in his arms. She lifted her mouth to kiss the spot beneath his chin then laid her head against his broad chest.

"Last night was incredible," Kendrick said.

She nodded. "It was. You were amazing."

"You and I are amazing together," he whispered softly.

Lifting her head Vanessa scanned his face.

"I don't know what I'm going to do with you," Kendrick said as he stared into her eyes. "You've really got my head twisted, Vanessa."

She smiled. "Is that a bad thing?"

He tightened the hold he had on her, his embrace comforting. He just held her, not bothering to respond. With his hands in her hair he tilted her mouth to his and kissed her deeply. His tongue pushed past her lips, need and want urging him on. His hands moved softly over her back, caressing her until she appeared almost too weak to stand. He suddenly wanted her under him and he said so as he lifted her in his arms. Reaching for the shower handle behind them he shut off the water.

Kendrick carried her back to the bedroom, where he laid her on the bed. He stared, unable to take his eyes off her. Kneeling above her he dropped his mouth to her breast and sucked her nipple between his lips. He licked the dampness from her skin, bathing the rock-candy protrusion with his tongue. He used his finger and thumb on the other, kneading it gently. Vanessa squirmed with excitement.

When he'd fully serviced one breast he moved to the other. He was learning her body well and knew he could bring her to orgasm just by playing with her nipples.

His mouth was hot and wet against her flesh and she sucked in swiftly at the sensation of his touch. His teeth grazed the nipple and she moaned loudly. She was on fire and he was purposely taunting her sensibilities.

He suddenly pulled his mouth from her, easing his body down as he straddled his legs around her. He slid down the length of her body, pulling one leg up and then the other. He pushed her knees open until she was spread wide, her legs open like the expanse of a butterfly's wings.

He slid down until his lips grazed her inner thigh. Vanessa gasped, then whimpered as she clutched the blankets beneath her body. Kendrick extended his body between her legs as he eased his arms behind her knees, pulling her to his mouth. He inhaled the scent of her, her desire fueling his own as his erection extended like a concrete bar. He pressed a gentle kiss against one thigh and then the other. Then he licked her, his tongue trailing over her clit. The nub was throbbing for attention. He licked her slowly, his touch teasing. He licked her, tasting her secretions as she pushed herself into his mouth. She was deliciously sweet as he thrust his tongue into her. Her hips jutted upward and she groaned in pure, unadulterated pleasure.

Vanessa moaned and begged him for more, unable to resist the desire surging through her. She was desperate for release, tears rolling down her cheeks. His tongue flicked her clit and lips, fast and slow, again and again. She couldn't keep still and he held her tightly. Before she realized what was happening he rolled, flipping her body above his. She was suddenly riding his face as he sucked her throbbing clit into his mouth. She wrapped her hands around his head, pulling him into her crotch as she bucked her hips against his face.

Vanessa cried out as he continued to nibble at her private parts. She called out his name, over and over again as if she were in prayer. She tensed as his tongue thrust inside her, the sweetest pressure against her love button. He licked and rubbed faster and faster and then he plunged his fingers into her. Her body exploded at the infraction, her juices flooding into his mouth. With each spasm she ground herself against his face, her body quivering with pleasure as she bucked hard against his tongue. Her body rocked back and forth, shuddering as every nerve ending reacted with pleasure. Kendrick continued to lick her dry. Easy passes of his tongue and gentle whispers of warm breath until she was too sensitive to be touched more. She pulled her body from his grasp, collapsing above him.

Needing his own release Kendrick kissed her thighs, the line of her pubic hair, her belly button. As he reached for a condom he'd rested on the nightstand, he spied the look of pure satisfaction that blessed her face and his member hardened even more. Her eyes were closed and her breathing was heavy as he crawled up to lie beside her, his body extended alongside hers. He sheathed himself quickly before pulling her into his arms. He rolled himself above her, easing himself swiftly between her legs.

It was sweet torture as he teased her flesh with his own. She arched ever so slightly as he entered her, his body melting into hers. She wrapped her arms around his neck, her hands playing in his hair. Everything about them together felt perfect, immensely so, and Kendrick didn't want it to ever end. He loved how she felt, loved the sounds she murmured against his ear. And as both their bodies convulsed with pleasure he realized that what he was feeling for her was love.

"No," he said, gasping for air as he finally answered her question. "No. It's not a bad thing at all."

Vanessa couldn't have been happier. The days were flying by and she and Kendrick played house for most of them. Conversation between them was easy as they continued to discover more about each other. She loved that they shared a penchant for all things sports-related, action movies and hot wings. Kendrick's boast that his home-cooked hot wings would easily outdo hers had been the catalyst for another bet and she was already plotting how to ensure she would win.

They had spent time walking the beach hand in hand, impressed by the staff, who'd removed all remnants of the previous week's storm. The sand was pristine, every leaf and tree limb gone. As they'd taken short strolls around the island to assess the damage, they found no more evidence of the destruction the hurricane had caused. The patio furniture was back in place and even the flora was full and abundant, with no trace of the high winds that had sapped them to shreds. And when the sun had been sky-high, the temperatures rising as rapidly, they'd gone swimming in the ocean waters and then the infinity pool. Every day was a lazy day, and more times than not, Vanessa had forgotten why they were there in the first place.

Vanessa appreciated his sense of humor and Kendrick made her laugh until her sides ached. When they weren't talking and laughing, they were making love. She'd lost count of the number of times she'd climaxed in his arms. Every day had been a good day. Falling asleep beside him had become the most natural thing for her to do.

It had been twelve days since the first time they'd made love. Twelve days of pure pleasure. And when Kendrick had disappeared to run an errand she had planned a romantic dinner, conspiring with Liam to plate all of his favorite foods: fried chicken, collard greens, corn bread and apple pie. She asked for the meal to be served by the pool, complete with candlelight and flowers and his favorite craft beer. Liam's assurances that everything would be perfect had fueled the excitement that still consumed her.

Standing in the walk-in closet she flipped through the dresses inside, trying to find the perfect one to celebrate their dinner. They were all cute and his sister had done a good job finding things for her to wear but the perfect dress for the romantic evening she hoped to have wasn't there. She wanted something sexy, classic and fitted that would hold his attention. Searching out pen and paper she wrote Kendrick a quick note, grabbed her purse and headed out to the resort's shopping strip.

Kendrick tossed a quick look over his shoulder, his hand on the doorknob. Once he was certain that no one had seen him, he opened the door and let himself in. The four men inside greeted him warmly.

There was Simon Brandt, Kent Jessup, Mike Terrence and Liam, all trusted members of his team. Each came with impressive résumés: two were former members of a paramilitary group, one was a technology specialist, and another, a retired navy SEAL. All of them had combat and weapons training and they were friends, having served together longer than they hadn't. Together with Zak Sayed they had gotten each other out of some sticky situations and Kendrick trusted the lot with his life.

"Yo, boss man!"

"Hey, boss."

"Boudreaux, baby!"

Liam waved a chicken leg in his direction. "Playa! How's it hangin'?"

He shook his head. "Chicken? Really?"

"Your girl is putting the chef through some things. She wants old-fashioned Southern-fried chicken for your dinner tonight. I was just taste-testing, making sure it's perfect."

"I want fried chicken," Kent Jessup said. He was tall, with blue eyes, blond hair and the build of a wide receiver.

"We all want some fried chicken!" Mike chimed.

Kendrick shook his head. "So, where are we at?" he said.

Liam took a bite of his chicken leg and pointed at the redhead in the group. "Simon's been watching the movies on your girl's cloud account."

Simon nodded. "Hacking her account was a breeze. She really needs to be a little more creative with her passwords. I've transferred all of her data to a secure server. If he figures out she has a cloud account there won't be anything on it when he goes to look. But Ms. Harrison is really good. She's got a great eye. Some of these films are quite entertaining."

"You find anything yet that we can use?" Kendrick asked.

He shook his head. "Nothing out of the ordinary. Your boy Bennett kept trying to get closer to her but she kept shutting him down. Hard! He didn't take it lightly, either. She caught him on camera when he didn't know it. He's got a temper. But your girlfriend was cold. It even hurt my feelings a time or two!"

The others laughed.

Simon typed something on his keyboard and the video he'd been watching popped up on all the screens in the room.

It was a panoramic view of Marcus Bennett's boat. The party was wild and the guests were live. The booze was flowing like water and the music was loud. Kendrick recognized the late Alexandra and Paolo Medina from the family photographs that had been in their Miami home. The couple was having a good time and they looked happy.

Marcus Bennett suddenly appeared in the camera's screen, moving in the filmmaker's direction. The camera's view dropped to the wooden deck, capturing her manicured toes and his sneakered feet. Their conversation was short and sweet, him inviting her to join him below deck and Vanessa politely declining. Bennett had persisted but Vanessa had stood her ground. The camera had followed as he'd stormed off in the other direction.

Vanessa had zoomed in as he'd stood with two of his cronies. He'd shot her a dirty look and there was no missing his vile comment that had his associates bent over in laughter. The camera scanned the crowd a second time. When it returned to Marcus, two other men had joined him. Kendrick suddenly bristled.

"Pause that and zoom in," he said, moving to Simon's side.

"Well, I'll be damned," Kent crooned as the enlarged image came into view.

"Holy Toledo," Mike chimed.

"What?" Simon questioned as they watched a monetary exchange happen between Bennett and the two well-dressed men.

Kendrick shook his head. "The better question is why. Why would a United States senator and a congressman be in the presence of a known criminal? And what business did they have together that required them to pay Bennett in cash?"

"A lot of cash, too," Simon chimed. "Two briefcases full. Looks like your girlfriend stepped into something deeper than just Marcus."

"Keep digging," Kendrick said, purposely ignoring the girlfriend comment. "Looks like we're onto something. Anything else I need to know?"

"We had a plane land this morning," the other man said, his fingers dancing over the computer keyboard as his gaze focused on a screen. "I'm still running background checks on the crew and passengers. Two couples checked in today—Mr. and Mrs. Paul Malone, and David and James Pritchard-Smith."

Kendrick nodded. "Keep me posted. Anything come in from home base?"

Mike shook his head. "Radio silence. But there's been some serious chatter across the network. Whatever this is, Bennett wants all evidence of it. And he wants it bad."

"Enough to come looking for it?"

The man nodded. "Leaking her whereabouts has definitely drawn him out of hiding."

Kendrick took a deep breath and held it. It had been his idea to use Vanessa as bait to lure Marcus Bennett to them. Once they'd gotten intel that she had something the fugitive feared law enforcement would find first, it made perfect sense. With their ability to keep everything contained, the island had been the ideal ruse. Purposely putting her in the line of danger had come with some reservations but he trusted the men who stood in that room with him. They were all the best of the best and good at their respective jobs. He also knew Marcus Bennett's type. The man was arrogant and didn't like to be beaten. Kendrick was certain he would come for Vanessa. He just didn't know when. As he reflected on everything he knew and even a few things he wasn't too certain about, he suddenly found himself second-guessing himself. Liam must've seen it on his face.

"Yo, boss! We still good to go?"

He met the look the man was giving him as all of them turned to get a read on his mood. Blowing the breath past his lips Kendrick nodded. "Yeah, we're good."

Liam grinned. "Just checking. You and that little filly have gotten pretty close these past few weeks. In fact, that do-not-disturb sign is on the door all night and half the day."

Mike, Simon and Kent all laughed, the trio high-fiving each other like college frat boys.

Kendrick cut his eye at his friends. "We still have a job to do, gentlemen. Y'all just stay focused, please."

Mike suddenly snapped his fingers as he scanned the computer in front of him. "Uh, Houston, we have a problem."

Kendrick bristled. "What's wrong?"

Mike turned in his direction, a wide grin across his face. "The baby done got out of the cradle, Mr. Baby-sitter. I just got a hit on your girl's credit card. Looks like she done bought herself a new dress!"

Chapter 12

Vanessa loved the new dress she'd just purchased. It was cute and sexy and as excited as she was for Kendrick to see her in it, she was even more anxious for him to get her out of it. Her face flushed with color as the thought crossed her mind.

She waved a quick goodbye to the shopkeeper. As she made her exit thoughts of Kendrick were still racing through her mind. She suddenly came to an abrupt stop when she spied a pair of designer shoes in the store next door. The red-bottomed pumps were stylish, the minimalistic lines classic, and the snake-skinned upper was extraordinary. Vanessa's eyes widened at the distraction.

Inside the shoe store, Vanessa's excitement gleamed on her face. The salesclerk was eager to please and it took no time at all before Vanessa was trying on that shoe and a few others. As she strolled from one side of the room to the other, another shopper remarked on the high heels she was modeling.

"Those are too cute!" the woman said, stopping to admire Vanessa and her shoes.

Vanessa grinned. "Aren't they, though!"

"I can see those with a pencil skirt and button-up blouse. It would be classic!"

Vanessa nodded her agreement, lifting her eyes to study the woman talking to her.

"My name's Lydia," the woman said. "And you look very familiar. Have we met before?"

Lydia was long and lean, a tall leggy brunette with a large bustline and thin waist. Her features were mannish, hard and chiseled. She wore a casual jogging suit and expensive Nike sneakers.

Vanessa hesitated for a brief moment, something about the woman's countenance giving her reason to pause. "I don't think so. But it's nice to meet you, Lydia. My name's…" She suddenly hesitated. "My friends call me *Mattie*," she said.

Lydia smiled. "Well, it's nice to meet you, Mattie. My husband, Paul, and I just got in today. We renewed our vows and this is our much-deserved getaway."

For the first time Vanessa noticed the man standing against the wall, his arms crossed over his chest. Lydia's husband was short and bullish with a ruddy complexion. The duo looked like an unlikely pairing and Paul didn't look happy to be there.

Vanessa nodded. "Well, I hope you both have a great time. It's a beautiful island."

"So, who are you here with?"

Before Vanessa could respond Kendrick came through the front door. His eyes shifted quickly around the room as he moved to her side. He wrapped an arm around her waist and lightly kissed the top of her head. "Hey, you," he said softly.

Vanessa smiled as she directed her comment at the other woman. "I'm here with my husband." She leaned to kiss Kendrick's mouth as she slid into his side. "Honey, this is Lydia and her husband, Paul."

Kendrick extended his hand in greeting. "Hi. Nice to meet you both."

Paul shot him a quick nod but he said nothing. Lydia shook Kendrick's hand enthusiastically.

"So, you done shopping?" Kendrick asked, dropping his gaze to Vanessa's face.

She nodded. "I just need to pay for my shoes," she said as she passed her credit card to the cashier.

Kendrick reached past her to pull the card from the sales associate's hands. He slid his own in its place. "My treat," he said to Vanessa as he handed her credit card back to her.

"Thank you," she said, surprise shining in her eyes.

"Good-looking and generous," Lydia exclaimed as she watched him sign the credit card receipt. "A man after my own heart."

"It was nice to meet you," Vanessa said as she gathered her bags and Kendrick took her hand.

Lydia took a step forward and Kendrick bristled.

Vanessa could feel his body tense and her own stiffened in response.

"I was wondering," the woman said, her voice dropping to a loud whisper as she came to a stop in front of them. "Do you two swing, by chance?"

Confusion washed over Vanessa's expression. "Swing?"

Lydia nodded. "Paul and I like to play when we come here and we're always excited when we meet couples who want to play with us."

Kendrick shook his head. "Sorry, Lydia. There's only one woman I play with and that's my wife. And I'm not too keen on her playing with anyone else."

"Well, I just had to ask. We could have had a lot of fun," she said as she reached out to draw her finger against Vanessa's arm.

Vanessa leaned closer to Kendrick, flinching slightly in his embrace. They watched as Lydia moved back to Paul's side, focusing her attention on a pair of high heels in the display case. With an arm still holding tight to her, Kendrick led them to the door. As he and Vanessa stepped through the exit he tossed one last look over his shoulder. Both Lydia and her husband had turned to watch them leave, their expressions indifferent.

Kendrick's own gaze narrowed suspiciously, his instincts telling him the couple and their alternative lifestyle were more than what they appeared.

Back in their bungalow, behind the locked bedroom door, Kendrick shook his head in her direction. "Baby, did it cross your mind that you can be traced through your credit card?"

Vanessa's eyes widened. "I didn't think…"

He held up his hand. "You really should have asked me first," he said.

"I left you a note," she said, pointing to the message that rested on the bedspread at the foot of the bed.

He sighed. It bothered him that he had to appear angry when she was doing exactly what they had wanted her to do. Ensuring Marcus Bennett could easily track her down had been exactly what they'd needed. But now that danger had potentially reared its head, Kendrick found himself questioning his motivations and the risks. He turned away from her. He couldn't chance her reading the emotion that crossed his face.

"Does this mean we have to leave?" she questioned. "Did I really mess up?"

He turned back to her, hearing the sudden shakiness in her voice. He then closed the space between them. He took her into his arms and kissed her forehead. "It's all good," he said. "If it becomes a problem we'll know soon enough."

She nodded her head against his chest. "I don't know what I was thinking!"

He clasped her face between his hands and kissed her mouth. A tear fell from her eyes and he kissed that away. "Don't cry. You look like a chipmunk when you cry."

Vanessa laughed. "I do not!"

"Yes, you do." His head moved up and down against his shoulders.

Vanessa rolled her eyes and took a deep breath. "So what now?" she questioned.

Kendrick smiled. "Now you go put on your pretty

new dress and shoes and let's have a wonderful dinner," he said.

He leaned and kissed her and in that moment it took everything in him not to tell her all that was going on. Instead he hugged her close, then spun her about. With a tap on her backside he pushed her toward the bathroom. With a quick glance over her shoulder Vanessa blew him a kiss then disappeared into the other room.

Exiting the bedroom Kendrick gestured for Liam's attention. The man and a team of five other resort staff were transforming the space for dinner. Kendrick was impressed with the changes that had already taken place but he didn't have the time to pay it any real attention.

The two men locked gazes as Kendrick held up his index finger. Easing down the short length of hallway he made sure Vanessa was in the shower and unable to hear their conversation.

"You were right," Liam whispered. "We don't know who they are yet but they are not Lydia and Paul Malone."

"Neither one of them is Marcus Bennett, either. So why are they here?"

"We're all on it," Liam said.

Kendrick nodded. In the distance they both heard the shower stop. He gestured for Liam to go back to his task. "I need to change for dinner," he said.

Liam nodded. "I'll let you know as soon as I know more," he said as he eased back out to the patio.

Vanessa suddenly peeked her head out the door. "Hey, was someone at the door?"

Kendrick nodded. "Liam was just checking in with

us. They're setting up for dinner. There's a lot going on out here."

She nodded. "What did you tell him?"

He smiled. "I told him we'd be dressed and ready in another hour or so." He held up the do-not-disturb sign, hanging it over the knob of the bedroom door.

Vanessa grinned. "Sounds like we need to work up an appetite, then," she said.

Kendrick laughed as he moved into the bedroom and locked the door behind them. "That's exactly what I was thinking!"

Kendrick was in complete and total shock when he exited the bedroom. The staff had completely transformed the living space and it suddenly looked like Christmas. White lights decorated the ceilings, running from inside the space to the canopy outside. There was an oversize Douglas fir tree in the corner of the living room adorned with miniature white lights, multicolored bulbs and strands of garland made from fresh flowers. The lights had been dimmed in the room and a fire burned in the fireplace. Outside, lights decorated the palm trees and massive pots of red-berried holly had been situated on the flagstone tiles. The mood was festive and the tropical setting felt very much like the holiday. He suddenly found himself excited for Vanessa to experience the transformation.

Liam was standing at attention when Vanessa finally made an appearance, her eyes flitting back and forth as she took in the view. He held one hand behind his back, the other in front of him, his requisite towel

hanging pristinely. Kendrick had been seated but came
to his feet as she moved to his side.

She looked exquisite and his eyes widened at the
sight of her. She wore a beaded cocktail dress, the hem
falling just above her knees. The dress was sleeveless
with a round neckline and the stretch mesh foundation
was adorned with hand-sewn beads that shimmered
with color. The back was open, cut low against the
curve of her buttocks, and the garment complemented
every dip and curve of her luscious frame. With her
hair pulled into a loose chignon atop her head and her
meticulous makeup, she was absolutely stunning. Even
Liam's eyes widened at the sight of her.

She pressed a palm to his chest as she leaned up to
give him a kiss. As Kendrick kissed her back he was
oblivious to everything else around them. When he finally came up for air he didn't miss the side-eyed look
his associate was giving him, the man fighting not to
break out into an approving grin. Kendrick followed
Vanessa around the table to pull out her seat.

"You look incredible," he whispered once they were
seated across from each other.

Vanessa smiled brightly, the gesture illuminating
her face. "Thank you."

They sat staring at each other as Liam moved from
one to the other, filling their glasses and serving the
meal.

"Does everything meet with your approval, madam?"

She nodded enthusiastically. "It does. Thank you
so much for everything you did to make this happen,
Liam. The decorations are perfect."

"Your wish is my command, madam. Is there anything else I can do for you now?"

Kendrick shook his head. "No, thank you."

"Enjoy your meal, sir," Liam said as he slipped out of the room.

The food was reminiscent of home and Kendrick made a mental note to call his family as soon as he had a moment alone. Vanessa had gone above and beyond to have all his favorites served. The chicken was seasoned and fried to perfection. The corn bread was light and moist with a hint of jalapeno and the apple pie with its buttery, flaky crust all melted in his mouth. Whatever she'd put the chef through had been well worth the effort.

"This was incredible," he said as he swiped the cloth napkin across his lips. "The fried chicken was almost as good as my mother's."

"I'm so glad," she said. "I was nervous."

He leaned back in his seat, folding his hands together in his lap. "You never did tell me what we're celebrating," he said, eyeing her curiously.

She smiled. "I just wanted to enjoy you forgetting about your job for a minute."

Kendrick laughed. "Woman, I think I forgot about my job that first time I kissed you!"

She laughed with him. "Maybe, but it's nice to acknowledge that you didn't get all weird about it."

He nodded. "You're right. It's not every day I risk being unemployed to be with a woman who's got my head all twisted. I think I'm handling it pretty well."

Vanessa sat straighter in her seat. "All twisted?" she repeated.

His smile was easy. "Yeah. You've got me in a jam, Ms. Harrison. I'm not sure what I'm going to do with you."

Vanessa dropped her gaze into her lap and when she lifted her eyes back to his, he was still staring at her. "Do you think you could love me?" she asked, her voice dropping to a whisper.

Kendrick stared at her, saying nothing. The silence was formidable.

Finally Kendrick rose from his seat and moved to her side. Extending his hand out to her he pulled her onto her feet, drawing her into his arms. The music playing in the distance was soft and seductive, echoing into the space. Wrapping himself around her he hugged her close and began to slow-dance with her beneath the full moon. He held her for some time, still not bothering to answer her question. And when Liam came to serve the dessert, interrupting the moment, Kendrick still hadn't found the words to tell her that he already did.

Chapter 13

Vanessa's eyes fluttered open and then closed as she willed her body awake. As her eyes adjusted to the darkness she saw a shadowy figure standing at the foot of the bed. She sat upright, backing against the pillows. Liam stood staring at her, a gun pointed at her heart. Panic suddenly gripped her and she screamed, calling out for Kendrick to come save her.

Vanessa's screams pulled Kendrick from a sound sleep. He jumped, flipping on the light next to the bed. She was writhing from side to side, her forehead beaded with perspiration. He called her name as he shook her awake, pulling her from the hold of a frightening nightmare.

Her eyes suddenly flew open, her gaze skating from side to side. She was panting for air, her heart beating harshly in her chest . Comfort came when Kendrick pulled her into his arms, whispering lightly against her ear.

"Shh, it's okay. It was just a bad dream," he said, his gentle tone consoling.

Vanessa clung to him, her breathing still erratic. "He was standing at the foot of the bed and he had a gun," she finally sputtered.

Kendrick shook his head, concern furrowing his brow. "Who? Who had a gun?"

"That damn butler!"

Kendrick smiled. "The door's locked, baby. There was no one in the room with us. And definitely not Liam."

"Are you certain?"

"Positive. It was only a dream."

Vanessa hesitantly settled her body down against his. "It just felt so real," she said.

He kissed her cheek as he laid his body back down, pulling the covers back over his shoulders. "Go back to sleep," he whispered. "I'm right here and I'm not going anywhere."

Nodding, Vanessa reached to turn off the light and snuggled her body back down against his. Within minutes Kendrick was sound asleep again, snoring softly against her ear. The lull of his breathing was soothing and she allowed herself to relax. As she lay beside him she thought back to their evening together. Kendrick had never answered her question and she wondered if he just didn't want to hurt her feelings by saying no. Maybe he couldn't see himself loving her.

She was foolish to think that there could be anything between them. Despite the physical connection they shared, which was fueled by the romantic setting and close proximity they found themselves in, he really didn't know her at all. And she didn't know him. Her life was in New York and his was tied to the secrets of the government agency he serviced. She had no right to expect that their time together was more than it was. She had no right to expect anything at all from him. So how could she expect him to love her?

But she did. She wanted him to love her as much as she felt herself loving him. And she did love him. Kendrick had captured her heart and was holding it hostage. She loved him with every fiber of her being and she wanted him to share the same emotion she did.

Between the dreams and her own frustrations, Vanessa had not slept well. She had tossed and turned most of the night, contemplating every possible scenario that she and Kendrick could find themselves in. As she stood in the shower, the water raining over her face, she ran through her list again.

Kendrick could realize he loved her and they could live happily ever after. He could go his way and she could go hers and their time together would be a sweet memory to draw on in her old age. Marcus could shoot her dead and put her out of her misery. She shook her head at the absurdity.

When she stepped out of the shower she heard Kendrick in the bedroom. He was talking to his mother and that made her smile. As he ended the call, telling the woman that he loved and missed her, tears misted her eyes. He was sitting on the edge of the bed as she entered the room.

"Good morning," she said, meeting his stare.

Kendrick nodded. "Good morning."

"How was your run?"

"It was good. I ran an extra mile today."

She smiled. "I think we need to talk," she said, a wave of anxiety sweeping through her body.

Kendrick tilted his head as he eyed her. She was clutching an oversize towel tightly around her body. Rivulets of water rolled over her face and shoulders. Her knees were locked tightly together and her body language reflected her nervousness.

He lifted his hand and beckoned her to him with one finger. He could see the hesitation in her eyes as she shifted her weight from one foot to the other. He raised an eyebrow at her. She took a deep breath, clearly pondering her options, before taking one tentative step toward him and then another. When she stopped before him, an arm's length away, her eyes were glued to the floor, fighting not to look at him.

Kendrick continued to stare at her. He rose from his seat and stepped toward her, closing the short distance between them until they were nearly touching. He brought his hand to her chin, lifting her face to his. "What do you want to talk about?" he asked as his fingers gently caressed the side of her face.

Distracted by the nearness of him Vanessa stammered foolishly, her next words completely lost. The front of his shorts had tented, exposing the rise of an erection, and she found herself struggling not to stare. She took a deep breath, inhaling the scent of him. He smelled like a man and it was the sweetest aphrodisiac. She closed her eyes and imagined it pulsing for her attention. Pure decadence filled her thoughts.

She finally opened her eyes and looked up at him. His smile was slight and endearing. It felt like an eternity that they stood gazing into each other's eyes.

Kendrick wrapped his arms around her, pulling her into a tender embrace. His erection crushed between them and Vanessa felt herself grinding her body against him. Her gyrations were slow and easy. She drew her hands to his chest, her palms pressing against his torso. He hugged her tighter, his arms encircling her as he leaned into her neck. Nuzzling his nose against her he breathed in deeply.

Vanessa's hands trailed down to his waist as she wrapped her arms around him. He let out a breath he didn't know he'd been holding and pulled her even closer. Tilting his head he kissed her neck, her cheek, blowing warm breath against her earlobe. The sweetest whimper eased past her lips.

Kendrick snatched the towel she'd been clutching and Vanessa gasped loudly as he pulled it from her body and let it drop to the floor beneath their feet. He eased his hands down her back and felt her tremble with anticipation. He stopped at the rise of her buttocks, his fingers caressing the tight curve of her bottom. As he pulled her pelvis to his own he leaned to capture her mouth, covering it with his own.

Vanessa pressed her hands to his chest, pushing slightly as she tried to regain a semblance of control. Her efforts were feeble. Her body was reacting on its own accord, her mind focused on nothing but his touch. As if reading her mind Kendrick tightened his hold. His mouth continued to dance over hers as her lips parted enough for him to snake his tongue inside.

She tasted like the minty mouthwash on the counter in the bathroom. He stroked her tongue, reveling in its tenderness. He felt her swallow as his tongue invaded her mouth, searching for the back of her throat. His kiss was intense, passionate and anxious. And he kissed her until he felt her knees buckle.

She was light in his arms and he held her up easily. Her hands moved from his chest to his arms and she clung to him as if he was a lifeline and she feared ever letting go. Her chest heaved up and down against his. Tiny whimpers converged into low, throaty moans. She melted against him, her tongue entwining with his. Kendrick groaned into her mouth as they stood there making out like teenagers.

Breaking the embrace he leaned back so that he could look into her eyes. His pelvis was still pressed firmly against hers, the rise of his manhood begging for release. Her eyes were closed, her mouth parted, and her body trembled with anticipation.

Vanessa's skin was on fire and when she opened her eyes, her brows climbing toward her hairline, the look she gave him was telling.

Desire seeped from her intense stare, burning heat straight through him. Kendrick grabbed her hand, entwining his fingers with hers. He stepped back, pulling her along with him until his legs hit the bed and he sat down, drawing her between his legs. Needing to feel her against him he slid his T-shirt off, tossing it aside. His breathing became ragged as she roamed her hands over his chest and across his broad back. He closed his eyes, basking in her gentle caresses. He was beyond aroused, his organ so ridiculously hard he felt as if a steel beam had grown in his shorts. Kendrick leaned back, propping himself up with his arms as Vanessa cavorted freely, her soft hands gliding like silk across his chest, shoulders, stomach, arms and legs, ignoring the protrusion against his inner thigh. It was beautiful agony. A low sigh escaped past his lips.

Leaning forward he pulled her against him, pressing his lips to her cheeks, then her mouth, planting damp kisses on each eyelid, then her forehead. He kissed and licked and nibbled a trail down her neck and along her profile. His hands slid around her waist and gripped each one of her butt cheeks. He pulled her on top of him and rolled her onto her back. He began to devour her, suckling one nipple and then the other. His kisses were easy and gentle as he worked his mouth and tongue across her heated skin. He kissed his way back up to her mouth, sliding his tongue back where it belonged as he crushed his body against hers.

Kendrick couldn't remember ever wanting a woman as much as he found himself wanting Vanessa. His desire was all consuming, more need than craving. He needed to feel every pore, every hair follicle, to literally merge every ounce of his entire body into hers. It was a sweet ache, her radiance nourishing everywhere they touched.

Vanessa pulled herself from him, pushing herself backward till her back hit the pillows. Kendrick instinctively crawled up after her. He lay down against her, pinning her beneath him as he continued to engulf her mouth, assailing her tongue with his tongue.

He lost track of time as they explored each other, rolling back and forth against each other. Her mouth and hands made him squirm. He gasped and moaned when her tongue slid against his nipples, his neck, his clavicle, her teeth nipping at him with each pass. She gently kissed her way down his chest, over his abs, dipping her tongue into the well of his belly button.

She reached her hands past the waistband of his running shorts. She pulled them and his underwear off in one masterful tug that made Kendrick smile. His boy parts greeted her eagerly as she hovered over him. Reaching for a condom on the nightstand she continued to trail kisses over his face and torso. As she sank down onto him his cock drooled with want as his natural instincts kicked in.

With both hands clutching her breasts, his fingers kneading her nipples, Kendrick was grinding himself in that warm place between her thighs. The path was slick and damp and with each thrust of his hips, her muscles tightened, drawing him in deeper and deeper. With each thrust he hit her sweet spot and she purred, the guttural sound feral.

"Oh, yes! Oh, yes!" she screamed, the only words

she'd spoken since he'd first touched her. "Oh, Kendrick, yes!"

Kendrick held her as she trembled, her body convulsing atop his. As her muscles spasmed, nerve endings trembling with pure pleasure, she suddenly found herself on her back, Kendrick plunging himself in and out of her. Her orgasm was an unending crescendo, relentless and unforgiving.

Kendrick drank in the sight of her, his eyes roving over her face. A hint of morning light peeking through the closed blinds kissed her cheeks and he became jealous, wanting all of her for himself. He was like a piston as he claimed her, jutting every ounce of himself into her. Pushing and pulling himself in and out of her he was like an avalanche, a tornado, a sexual force of nature. Beneath him, Vanessa began to frantically writhe and scream. She wrapped her legs around his waist and locked her heels behind his back. She was shaking, orgasmic bliss like a tidal wave washing over her.

And then Kendrick exploded. Her body felt magnificent wrapped around his as she milked him, each contraction of her velvet lining sending him over the edge of ecstasy. He could feel her heartbeat humming against his cock and he surged, convulsion after convulsion taking his breath away.

His body shook as hers trembled beneath him. He hugged her close as his body collapsed on hers. She nuzzled her face into his neck, her tongue giving him a gentle kiss. Kendrick cooed into her ear. Still lost deep inside of her he was unwilling to lose the connection as he shifted enough to swing her leg around so that she was spooning against him. She wiggled her bottom against his groin. He kissed her shoulder and the back of her neck, snaking his tongue against the lobe of her ear. With his arms around her he pulled her close to his chest and held her tightly. The words were there, *I love you* a whisper on his tongue, but before he could say them, they both drifted off to sleep.

Chapter 14

Kendrick stood along the edge of the shoreline, the satellite telephone pressed to his ear.

"What's going on, Sayed?" he asked. "My sister put you on a leash yet?"

Zak greeted him warmly. "Your sister is a special woman, Boudreaux. Very special."

Kendrick laughed. "So what's going down?"

"Base has some concerns."

"What's going on?"

"They can't seem to find your squad. Liam, Mike, Simon or Kent. Every one of them seems to have disappeared on leave."

"Huh!" Kendrick grunted, a smile crossing his face. "Imagine that."

"I told them they probably went on a boys' trip to

Vegas or something. Cards, booze and beautiful women. That kind of thing."

"That's probably what it is."

Zak chuckled softly. "I can't imagine it being anything else."

"Well, you know if I hear anything I'll let you know."

"I'm sure you will," Zak said.

There was a moment of pause before Zak spoke again, his tone suddenly serious.

"Word on the street is Marcus Bennett is about to make a move. Something has the man seriously on edge," Zak said.

"Do you know when it's supposed to go down?"

"Soon. Just keep your eyes open. He's shifting money and putting people in place. He's planning to hit and hit hard and they say he might even be on his way to Vegas."

Kendrick nodded into the receiver. "Good thing my team might already be there. I wouldn't want that son of a bitch to slip away."

"Watch your back, brother. Your sister's looking forward to spending time with you and Vanessa. Your mother, too."

Kendrick laughed. "How do they know I want to spend time with Vanessa?"

Zak laughed with him. "They know."

"So what do I get the twins for Christmas?" Kendrick asked, surfing the internet for gift ideas. "What do babies want from Santa Claus?"

Vanessa giggled as she moved to his side, dropping

down onto the sofa beside him. She pulled her legs beneath her bottom, sitting Indian-style. "They're babies. They're not going to remember what you get them."

Kendrick cut an eye at her. "I still need to get them something."

She pulled the laptop computer onto her lap. "There's this great baby site that sells the cutest moccasins for kids," she said as she typed in the web address.

"Moccasins?"

She nodded. "That and two savings bonds toward their college education would be great."

He nodded. "I like the savings bonds."

"They'll never get too many of them and the moccasins are just cute."

"Good! All the kids are taken care of. So what do I get my mother?"

Before she could answer Liam rushed into the room, pushing through the door without knocking. A sense of urgency painted his expression.

"Boss, we have an issue," he said, his gaze meeting Kendrick's.

Kendrick nodded. "Stay with Vanessa," he ordered.

Vanessa dropped the laptop onto the coffee table. "What's going on?"

Kendrick leaned to kiss her forehead. "Don't leave the bungalow," he said. "I'll be back to get you."

"But what's…" she started but Kendrick was out the door, leaving her and Liam alone. She turned her attention toward the uniformed man.

"What's going on, Liam?"

He crossed his hands together in front of himself.

"I'm sure Agent Boudreaux will be back soon, Ms. Harrison."

Her eyes widened. "You know my name?"

Liam smiled but he didn't bother to answer. Before she could ask another question Kendrick moved back through the door.

"There's no time," he said. "They're moving in too fast."

Liam's smile faded. "You're going to let it play out?"

"Everyone's in place."

"Would one of you please tell me what's going on?" Vanessa asked a second time.

Before either man could answer there was a knock on the door. She looked from Kendrick to Liam and back.

Kendrick moved to her side. "Do you trust me, Vanessa?"

Her gaze narrowed ever so slightly as confusion danced in her eyes. "Of course I trust you."

There was a second knock, harder and longer, someone anxious for their attention.

Kendrick nodded. "Then answer the door," he said.

She took a deep breath, moving slowly in the direction of the entrance.

Kendrick called after her. "And no matter what happens, Vanessa, remember that I love you."

Vanessa's head snapped as she turned to look at him. The rap against the door was harsher and he gestured for her to open it. Still staring at him, she reached for the knob and pulled it open.

The woman from the shoe store stood on the other side. "Hi, there! I'm sorry to bother you."

"Lydia, hey," Vanessa said. "What can I do for you?"

Lydia suddenly pulled a gun, pointing it in Vanessa's face.

"What? What's going on?" Vanessa stammered as she took two steps back.

Kendrick and Liam both bristled.

"Sit down," Lydia shouted, gesturing for Kendrick to take a seat.

Liam took a slight step back against the wall. His eyes never left Kendrick's face as the man slowly raised his hands and eased over to the sofa.

"What's this all about?" Kendrick asked.

A deep baritone voice rang in the entranceway. "This is all about respect," Marcus Bennett said. The man named Paul was behind him, holding his own gun in the air.

Vanessa gasped loudly, her breath catching in her chest. She felt herself begin to shake. "Marcus!"

Marcus's eyes skated around the room. He nodded at Liam, who nodded back. The gesture caught Vanessa by surprise and she tossed Kendrick a look. It took everything in her not to scream what she had told him before. The butler couldn't be trusted.

"Who's he?" Marcus asked, his eyes focused on Kendrick.

Lydia shrugged. "Her boyfriend."

Marcus smirked. "So now you have a boyfriend," he said, his gaze shifting back in Vanessa's direction.

"What do you want, Marcus?" she snapped.

He held up his index finger, waving it from side to

side. "Watch your tone, Vanessa. You don't want to make me angry."

She took a deep breath. "Just leave us alone. I didn't see anything."

He smiled. "You don't know what you saw," he said. "But you and that camera of yours have really gotten on my last nerve."

"I don't have my camera," she said. "It's in Miami."

Marcus nodded. He tossed Lydia a quick glance. "Lydia, did you find that camera in Miami?"

The woman nodded. "Yes, sir."

"What was on that camera?"

"Nothing, sir."

He looked back at Vanessa. "There was nothing on your camera, Vanessa. So I need to know what happened to the film you took on my yacht."

"I… It… I…" Vanessa stammered. She turned to look at Kendrick, who nodded his head slightly, his eyes locked on her face. She took a deep breath. "I saved it to my cloud account," she said.

Marcus nodded. "See how easy this is, Vanessa. I ask a question and you answer it."

A tear rolled down Vanessa's cheek.

Lydia grabbed the computer from the coffee table. She walked to the sofa table behind Kendrick and began typing furiously. "What's your password?" she said, lifting her eyes to Vanessa.

"My password? But that's not my computer," Vanessa said, confusion washing over her expression.

"To your cloud account," the woman snapped.

Vanessa's gaze shifted to Marcus, who tilted his

head. She stole a glance at Kendrick, whose eyes urged her on, and the five-digit code rolled easily off her tongue. Minutes passed before they all watched as Lydia downloaded file after file onto a flash drive. When she was done she moved to Marcus's side and handed him the tiny storage device.

"Did you delete all the files?" Marcus asked.

Lydia nodded. "Her cloud account doesn't exist anymore."

Marcus nodded. He pulled a cell phone from his pocket and placed a call. They all listened as he spoke quickly, instructions falling off his tongue. "If you find any trace of her cloud account I want to know," he said as he disconnected the call.

Vanessa cut her eye toward Lydia but the woman didn't seem to be fazed. She blew a low sigh. "What now?" she asked. "You have what you want."

The man's smile was smug and Vanessa would have given anything to slap the smirk off his face. "Now I'm going to leave. And when I'm gone your boyfriend is going to have a very nasty accident. I imagine your cute little love nest might even burn down and when the good butler here finds his body, they won't even be able to recognize him. It'll be quite a shame!" Marcus said.

"But you...I have something special planned for you," Marcus added, evil tinting his words. "I've already negotiated your sale to a very special friend. He likes to make pretty women feel a whole lot of pain. When he's done with you, you won't be so pretty anymore. Then he'll put you on the track to make him some money. You won't be saying no to his customers. In fact, you won't say no to another man ever again."

Vanessa was visibly shaking. She turned to stare at Kendrick, who was still sitting stoically, his expression emotionless. She turned back to find Marcus staring at her. The man eased his way to her side, standing in front of her. His gaze skated from the top of her head to her feet. He drew his fingers down the length of her arm and she stiffened, pulling away sharply from his touch.

"Don't touch her," Kendrick hissed between clenched teeth.

Marcus grinned, tossing him a look. "So, the boy-friend has finally found his *cojones*," he said.

Kendrick rose slowly, moving onto his feet, his hands still high in the air. Behind him, Paul raised his weapon and Lydia turned hers toward him, as well. "I didn't have to find them," he said, his tone snarky. "I never lost my balls."

Marcus eyed him warily, his gaze narrowing slightly. He held up his hand and both his lackeys lowered their weapons. "Don't kill him yet. A man should defend his woman even if she isn't worth the effort."

He suddenly grabbed Vanessa by the throat. His hold was harsh, his fingers digging deep into her skin. She gasped loudly as he cut off her air.

Behind him, Kendrick heard the hammer being cocked on that gun. Paul hissed in his ear as he pressed the barrel to the back of Kendrick's head. "Don't even twitch!" the man crooned.

With the last ounce of gumption she could find Vanessa spat, hurling a wad of foulness into Marcus's face.

He hurled her backward to the floor, swiping at the moisture that had landed on his cheek. Before anyone realized what was happening one shot and then a second fired through the air. At the same time, Kendrick hurled his body at Marcus, knocking him off his feet. He swung, a right hook, then a left, pummeling the man until he was down for the count.

When the first shot was fired Vanessa had rolled into a ball, her arms covering her head. She didn't budge until Kendrick was leaning above her, pulling her to her feet.

"Are you okay?" he asked, pulling her into his arms.

She was still shaking as she lifted her head, her gaze flying from one side of the room to the other. Liam was putting handcuffs on Marcus. Lydia was clutching her shoulder, blood spewing from a fresh wound. Paul was dead, his body folded over the back of the couch.

Two men she didn't recognize suddenly came through the door, one checking that Paul wasn't going to get back up and the other taking Lydia into custody.

Vanessa nodded her head.

"Nice shooting," Kendrick said, his comment directed at Liam.

The man's grin was a mile wide. "Almost missed that last one with you throwing your big head in front of the target."

Kendrick chuckled. "What about the others?" he questioned.

One of the newcomers nodded. "Signed, sealed and delivered. Even caught us a senator."

Vanessa's eyes shot around the room. "Please tell me what's going on. Who are these men?"

Kendrick gave her a tight squeeze. "This is my team. You know Liam. That there is Simon. The big guy is Kent, and you'll meet Mike a little later. He's putting the last bow on this package."

Vanessa dropped her face into her hands, swiping at the tears that were suddenly raining from her eyes. "I thought he was going to kill us."

Kendrick tossed a look in Marcus's direction. "Marcus thought he was going to kill us, but I wasn't planning on going out like that."

She glared at Liam. "I thought you were a bad guy."

"Sorry about that, little lady. But I will always have my boy's back," he said as he reached out to punch fists with Kendrick.

Vanessa's head was still swirling. She couldn't believe it was all over. That life could go back to normal. She sat against the edge of the pool as Kendrick answered her questions, filling in the missing details.

"You used me as bait?"

"I sent him on a wild-goose chase then I let him think he had found you."

"He could have killed me!" she exclaimed.

"The dead guy is a hired gun. He's got a rap sheet longer than your legs and was wanted in three countries. Once he showed up I knew Marcus didn't plan to do his own dirty work."

"But he shot that man in the club. He killed my friends!"

"They were fighting over territory. The man in the club caught him off guard. He was pushed into a corner and he couldn't show any weakness."

"So what happens to him now?"

"He's in federal custody. In a maximum-security prison. Bail has been denied so I expect that he's never going to see freedom again. He will never be a threat to you ever again."

"What about my movies?" she asked. "Did he really destroy everything?"

Kendrick chuckled softly. "He wiped out your account but we'd saved your files weeks ago."

She nodded. "So what was on them? Why were they so important to him?"

Kendrick reached a hand out to brush a strand of hair out of her eyes. "It's actually quite a scandal. Marcus supplied underage prostitutes to the senator and a group of his friends. You actually caught the congressman and one of the girls on tape. You also videotaped them paying off Marcus to keep it quiet. They were already under investigation and your film was pretty incriminating."

"What would you have done if Marcus hadn't come?"

Kendrick laughed. "I knew he'd come. You hurt his ego and he's all about his image. He had something to prove."

She tossed his comment around in her head then dismissed it. "I really thought Liam was a bad guy."

"I know. So did they. Liam fed them information we wanted them to have and they fell for it. That's why he works for me. He's good at his job."

There was a moment's pause as she took it all in,

sorting through the last few pieces of the puzzle. She shifted her body, turning to stare at him.

"What?" Kendrick questioned. "Why are you giving me that look?"

"You said you loved me."

He nodded. "I did."

She waited for him to say more but he didn't. But she didn't need him to say more. Knowing how he felt was more than enough. She took a deep breath, blowing it slowly past her lips. She reached for his hand, pulling his fingers to her lips. She kissed his palm, then folded his fingers into a tight fist, clutching it between both her hands. "So what now?"

Kendrick leaned in to kiss her mouth, allowing his lips to linger for a quick moment. As he pulled away he shrugged. "We still have to find a Christmas gift for my mother," he said.

Chapter 15

Gabrielle played quietly on the king-size bed as Vanessa finally unpacked her bags. She had been home for a few days, readjusting to life and no longer having to hide from Marcus Bennett. Kendrick had personally dropped her off, staying long enough to meet her parents. Over her mother's pork *carnitas* and lime margaritas, her father had expressed how much they appreciated everything Kendrick had done to protect her. He'd made quite an impression and her mother was still talking about him.

Saying goodbye to him had been the hardest thing Vanessa had ever done. He'd kissed her sweetly, wiping away her tears, and had promised that she would hear from him soon. Then he'd disappeared. That had been almost a week ago and she hadn't heard anything at all from him. She blew a deep sigh.

Gabrielle suddenly tossed a toy in her direction.

"Stop, Gabi," Vanessa snapped.

Gabrielle slung a second stuffed bear in her direction, the toy slamming her in the face.

"No, *chica*," Valeria Harrison-Braga scolded, moving into the room from the hallway. She shook her index finger at the little girl. "You do not be a bad girl," she said as she moved all of the toys out of Gabrielle's reach.

Gabi began to cry, muffling her sobs into a pillow. Vanessa rolled her eyes as she rubbed her cheek.

"Will you be a good girl?" Valeria asked. She patted Gabi against her back. The little girl sat back up and nodded her head as she swiped her eyes with the back of her hand. Valeria then nodded, returning one toy to Gabi's smiling face.

"You must have patience with her," Valeria said.

"She's a handful," Vanessa said.

Her mother nodded. "She has been through a lot. Now she needs some stability."

Vanessa dropped down onto the side of the bed. "So where are we with finding her grandparents?" she asked.

Valeria took a seat beside her. "That is what I want to talk to you about. Your brother found Paolo's parents. They are living in Bucerias, a small village north of Nuevo Vallarta."

"That's good!" Vanessa exclaimed. "They must be so excited."

Her mother shook her head. "Not so much," she said.

"The grandfather is very ill. They are old and their living conditions prohibit them from raising the child, even with the money Paolo left for them."

Vanessa blew a deep sigh. "So what now? What will happen to her?

Valeria tapped a thin hand against her daughter's knee. "Alexandra and Paolo designated you to be Gabrielle's guardian in the event his parents were unable to care for the child."

Vanessa's eyes widened. "Me? They wanted me to be responsible for her?"

Her mother nodded. "So it would seem. Your father's lawyer will explain it all to you."

Her mother rose to her feet. "Have you heard from that nice man?"

There was a brief moment of pause before she shook her head. "No. Kendrick hasn't called."

Valeria moved to the door. "Patience, daughter. I'm sure you will hear from him soon."

"He's a government agent, Mama. He was just doing his job."

"That might be so but he cares for you. And you have love for him, too."

Vanessa shrugged, unable to find the words to tell her mother just how much she loved Kendrick. She also preferred not to reveal just how much they'd shared in such a short amount of time.

Her mother spoke instead. "He is a good man, that one! Your father and I like Kendrick very much. I am certain that we will see him again." Turning, the woman moved out of the room.

As Vanessa pondered her mother's comments, Gabrielle moved against her back, wrapping her arms around Vanessa's neck. "Lub you!" she chimed, her tiny voice singing in Vanessa's ear. "Lub you, Nessa!"

Vanessa smiled. "I love you, too, Gabi."

Katherine Boudreaux wrapped her arms around her son's neck, hugging him warmly. "Congratulations!" she chimed, excitement shining across her face. "That was the perfect Christmas gift to give yourself!"

"Thanks, Mom," Kendrick said as he juggled the keys to his new home between his fingers.

"So, when are you moving in?" Maitlyn asked.

Kendrick shrugged. "I still have some things I need to take care of," he said. "Maybe sometime after the first of the year."

Maitlyn nodded. "Well, you know the minute Tarah and Kamaya find out they're going to start decorating."

Katherine shook her head. "You'll need to put the brakes on your sisters. No woman is going to want some other woman decorating her home."

Kendrick turned to stare at his mother. "What woman, Mama?"

His mother fanned her hand at him. "You know who I'm talking about. Vanessa. Don't act like you didn't buy that house for you and her to be living in."

Kendrick cut his eye at his sister, who lifted her hands, waving them defensively.

Katherine laughed. "Maitlyn didn't tell me about you and Vanessa. Zak spilled those beans."

Maitlyn laughed as her brother shook his head, his eyes rolling deep in his head.

"Mama, I don't know if Vanessa is going to move in with me," he said. He tossed his sister a look, his eyes pleading for a little assistance.

"Kendrick and Vanessa are still getting to know each other," Maitlyn interjected.

Katherine dropped her hands to her hips. "Oh, you know. And I'm telling you now, don't be living with that girl without the benefits of a marriage license. Your father and I won't have y'all shackin' up like you ain't been raised right. You love her so you better do right by her. Understand me?"

Maitlyn appeared as if she was fighting hard not to laugh.

Katherine repeated herself. "I said, do you understand me?"

"Yes, ma'am," Kendrick answered, feeling as if he'd just been scolded.

Katherine moved to his side and leaned to kiss his cheek. "I just knew we were going to marry Kamaya off before you," she muttered. "I don't know how I got that one wrong."

Maitlyn and Kendrick both burst out laughing as their mother made her way out of the room.

Kendrick pointed a finger at his sister. "I'm going to kill your husband," he said.

"I'm starting to think he needs to go back to work. He's definitely got too much time on his hands," Maitlyn teased.

The two laughed again, amusement dancing through the afternoon air.

Maitlyn shuffled through the pile of papers on the tabletop in front of her. "So, will you be with us for Christmas?"

Kendrick nodded. "That's the plan. I'm on hiatus for a minute. It's been a while since I've had some time off."

"What about Vanessa? Are you bringing her to Texas?"

Kendrick suddenly went quiet. He met the look his sister was giving him and shrugged his shoulders.

Maitlyn shook her head, annoyance crossing her face. "God, you men kill me! You haven't even called her since you got back, have you?"

"It's complicated," Kendrick said. "You wouldn't understand."

"Oh, I understand. You're having doubts. You're not sure if what you two shared was real. You had a great time together but you're wondering if it was only about the romantic setting and the stressful situation you were in. You're afraid that now that you two are back in the real world you won't be able to keep that momentum going. Am I close?"

There was a slight smile on Kendrick's face. "Did you inherit our mother's sixth sense? Or are you a mind reader now?"

Maitlyn laughed. "Let me tell you something. When my divorce became final I thought the world was going to end. I couldn't fathom being any sadder. Life got substantially better on that cruise. But when Zak left and I didn't hear from him those two months, I discovered what real unhappiness was. I felt like something inside me had died. I don't ever want to feel that again. I love him that much.

"Now, I can see it on your face that you miss her already. And if I'm right, Vanessa's experiencing the same unhappiness right now and she shouldn't have to. Trust your heart. It won't steer you wrong."

Kendrick nodded, swiping his eyes with his fingers. "Were you scared?"

Maitlyn laughed. "Hell yeah! I'd already had one relationship crash and burn. I didn't have a clue if I could survive another."

"So why'd you risk it?"

"Your boy stole my heart. Everything about the two of us together felt right. Just like it feels right with you and Vanessa."

He took another deep breath.

"So are you bringing Vanessa with you to Texas?" Maitlyn asked again impatiently. "I need to finalize our room needs at the ranch for Marah."

"And if I say yes?"

"Then you need to let me know if you want to share a room together or if you want her to bunk with Tarah, in which case I'll put you in a room with Donovan."

"Obviously, I'll need to see if she'll have me but put us down," he said as he nodded his head. "And I am not sleeping with Donovan. He snores."

Maitlyn smiled. "So what are you getting her for Christmas?"

"I have a few things in mind. What are you getting Mom?"

"Zak and I bought her a spa membership. It's one year of facials, manicures, pedicures and massages whenever she wants."

He nodded his approval. "I like that. Vanessa gave me a couple of ideas but I haven't gotten her gift yet."

"Do you want to know what I got Zak?" Maitlyn asked, her voice dropping to a loud whisper.

Kendrick smiled. "Oh, yeah! What could you possibly get the man who has everything?"

"He doesn't have everything," she said as she rose from the table. She moved to a collection of shopping bags that sat off in the corner of the room. She searched one and then another until she found a medium-size box, which she pulled into her hands. Moving back to the kitchen table she sat down, pushing the box in her brother's direction.

"I'm going to trust you to keep this a secret," she said, meeting his eyes.

Kendrick laughed. "If you want it to be a secret then I'm the *only* one you can tell," he teased.

Maitlyn laughed with him, watching as he pulled the top off the gift box and peered inside.

Tears suddenly pushed past his lashes. He cut his eye at her as he looked down at the object inside. "Really?" he whispered.

Maitlyn nodded, tears misting her eyes.

Kendrick pulled out a framed photo from inside. The black-and-white sonogram image looked like a large kidney bean with stubs for arms and legs. The silver frame was engraved with the words *Baby Sayed*.

"Do you know yet what it is?" he asked.

She shook her head. "Not yet. That was taken yesterday and I'm only six weeks along," she whispered back. "And you know I expect you to be our baby's godfather."

"So Zak doesn't know?"

"And you better not spoil my surprise," she said as she took the present from his hands and returned it to her hiding spot.

As she sat back down Kendrick leaned to wrap his arms around her. He hugged her close then kissed her cheek. "Congratulations. I am so happy for you!"

The two were still talking when Katherine made her way back into the room. "Maitlyn, I almost have your daddy's bags packed. I might need your help to get some of these presents packed if you have the time."

"No problem, Mom."

The matriarch nodded. "Kendrick, when are you and Vanessa getting to Dallas?"

Maitlyn laughed as Kendrick shook his head. "I'm not sure yet, Mama."

"I'm planning on doing Christmas Eve dinner. It'd be nice if all of us were together since you missed Thanksgiving with us."

"Yes, ma'am," Kendrick said, taking the hint.

After pouring a large glass of milk and filling a saucer with cookies, Katherine eased herself to the table and set the snack down in front of Maitlyn.

"What's this?" she asked, eyeing her mother curiously.

Katherine leaned to kiss her child's cheek, gently patting her abdomen. "You need to keep up your energy," she said, heading back out the door.

When she disappeared into the other room Kendrick locked gazes with his older sister. Maitlyn's eyes were wide, a look of astonishment on her face.

Kendrick shook his head. "I swear," he said, "nothing gets past our mother!"

Vanessa's arms were full with heavy shopping bags as she maneuvered her way into the family home. Last-minute Christmas shopping had taxed her nerves and she was past ready for the holiday to be over. She was half expecting Gabrielle to come running and when she didn't Vanessa had to wonder what the little munchkin was up to.

Her mother called her name, voices coming from the formal living room. "Vanessa, dear, we have a guest. Come say hello!"

Vanessa took a deep breath, rolling her eyes toward the ceiling. She'd grown weary of all the guests her mother had forced her to come say hello to. Her family had been entertaining friends and associates since she'd come home and despite her best efforts Vanessa didn't have any holiday spirit.

She moved to the hall closet, hung up her winter coat and tucked her purchases inside. Checking her reflection in the front hall mirror she took a deep breath and forced a smile onto her face.

Laughter rang warmly in the living space as Vanessa eased her way down the hall. Gabrielle was laughing, her little-girl chortle carefree and easy. Vanessa couldn't help but wish she felt as joyous.

Turning the corner into the room she saw her brothers first. Stephen and Shawn Harrison-Braga were both tall and thin, looking like identical clones of their father. Both turned as she entered the space, Shawn rushing to her side and sweeping her into his arms in a deep bear hug. Vanessa laughed heartily as she kissed one and then the other.

"I didn't think you two were coming for Christmas!" she exclaimed. She was genuinely excited to see them both, especially after discovering her parents had planned to fly to Mexico for the holiday, leaving her and Gabi alone.

Stephen shrugged. "We're not. We're headed to the Middle East for Christmas."

"I swear!" Vanessa exclaimed. "You two might as well live in Dubai. Every time I turn around that's where you are."

"Beautiful women will do that to you," Shawn teased.

Vanessa tossed her mother a look. "You said we had company. They aren't company."

Valeria nodded. "I wasn't talking about your brothers," she said as she pointed to the corner behind Vanessa.

Turning, Vanessa's eyes suddenly widened. Kendrick stood with Gabrielle in his arms, nuzzling the little girl's cheek. Her father was beside him, a wide grin across his face.

"Look!" Gabrielle exclaimed as she tightened her arms around Kendrick's neck. "Look, Nessa!"

Vanessa laughed, her eyes misting. "I see, Gabi! I see Kendrick!"

Gabrielle kicked her legs to get down. Once Kendrick placed the little girl on the floor she raced to Vanessa's mother, jumping into the woman's lap. "Eat, eat?"

Valeria nodded as she hugged the little girl to her. "That's a good idea, Gabrielle. Why don't you boys come into the kitchen with Gabi and me. I'm sure the cook has dinner ready by now, so we can all eat. Let's give your sister a little privacy with her friend." The woman moved to the door. "Kendrick, I hope you'll stay for dinner?"

Kendrick nodded. "I'd love to, Mrs. Braga."

Ambassador Braga shook Kendrick's hand. "I look forward to finishing our conversation," her father said. He leaned to kiss his daughter's cheek before making his exit, following behind his family.

The two stood staring at each other as the laughter moved down the hall to the other side of the family's home. Vanessa remained frozen, unable to believe that Kendrick was actually standing in the room with her.

"Hi," she finally whispered.

Kendrick closed the space between them, moving to her side. "Hi," he said as he eased an arm around her waist and gently pulled her to him.

Vanessa began to shake, tears welling in her eyes. She released the breath she'd been holding and gasped for air. "You didn't call me," she finally muttered.

He nodded. "I know. I came for you instead," he said.

"How long before you leave me again?"

"I'm not. When I go, you're going with me."

"Really? You want that?"

"I do, if you do. Do you?"

She took a deep breath, her eyes flitting from side to side. "I want forever, Kendrick. I don't want for the moment."

He chuckled softly. "I told you I loved you, remember?"

She nodded.

"I don't plan to say that to any other woman who isn't my mother or my sister. And I know I will never feel this way about any other woman except you."

Vanessa eased her arms around his neck. She was wearing flats so she rose up on her toes to press her cheek against his. "I love you, too," she whispered.

Kendrick held her, his lips dancing over her face. In that moment, she knew, beyond any doubts, that he would never let her go again.

Chapter 16

Noise and laughter rang throughout the Stallion home. Vanessa was in awe of all the activity that surrounded her. Even with everyone home, holidays with her family had never been quite so exuberant.

Katherine greeted her warmly, wrapping her in a deep hug. "It's so good to see you again, Vanessa," she said. "And look at that precious baby! It looks like she has grown since y'all were at my house." She gave Gabi a kiss on her cheek.

"It's good to see you, too, Mrs. Boudreaux, and thank you for inviting me to spend the holiday with you and your family."

Katherine waved a hand at Kendrick. "Find your sister or Marah. One of them will be able to tell you where you're sleeping. I need to get back into the kitchen to check on the food."

Kendrick kissed his mother's cheek. "It smells good. What are you cooking?"

"Seafood gumbo!" his mother exclaimed as she rushed off.

Kendrick shook his head. "Come on," he said as he pressed a wide palm against her lower back. "Let's see if we can find my sister."

Moving through the house Vanessa was thoroughly impressed. Briscoe-Stallion Estate was over eight hundred acres of working cattle ranch and an equestrian center. Back in the day, its original owner, Edward Briscoe, had been one of the first black cowboys. Since the expansion of Mr. Briscoe's longhorn operation, the family had added an entertainment complex that specialized in corporate and private client services. The property housed two event barns that were twenty-thousand square feet big, a country bed-and-breakfast and a wedding chapel. And the family home seemed to go on forever.

They peeked their heads into the formal dining room. Edward Briscoe, Senior Boudreaux and Matthew Stallion sat in discussion. Kendrick introduced her as he shook hands with his father and brother-in-law. "I think the women are out on the patio," Matthew said, pointing outside.

With a quick stop in the kitchen he introduced her to Edward's wife, Juanita, who, along with Katherine Boudreaux, was putting the final touches on the evening meal.

At an oversize, hand-hewn wood table John, Mark and Luke Stallion sat with Kendrick's brothers. They all greeted her warmly and she instantly felt comfortable. Continuing outside, they finally found Marah Stallion and Maitlyn.

Maitlyn embraced her warmly. "Hey, Vanessa! I'm so glad you came!"

"Thank you! I'm glad to be here, too," Vanessa replied, hugging her back.

Maitlyn introduced her to Marah.

"Just make yourself at home," Marah said. "We're very casual around here. And if you need anything, don't hesitate to ask."

"Thank you. I really appreciate that."

"So where do you want us to go?" Kendrick asked.

Marah gestured for them to follow her as she led the way to the second floor and the sleeping quarters. On their way she made a quick pit stop by the home's expansive playroom. The noise level increased tenfold, children screaming and running without a care in the world. Her eyes wide, Gabrielle practically leaped out of Kendrick's arms to get to the toys. She instantly bonded with a little girl in a pair of red cowboy boots.

"How old is she?" Marah asked.

"Not quite two," Vanessa answered.

"She's an absolute doll baby," Marah replied, a wistful look crossing her face.

"Hi, Irene!" Kendrick called, waving in the other child's direction.

Irene Stallion paused, eyeing him suspiciously. She

tossed him a dirty look, then turned back to Gabi, pulling the little girl behind her.

Marah laughed. "I don't know what it is, Kendrick, but Irene isn't feeling you."

Kendrick laughed with her. "You'd think I stole her lollipop or something," he said.

"They're all too cute," Vanessa said.

Marah pointed. "Irene is Mark and Michelle's little girl. The little one on the hobby horse over there is Jake."

"Jake is my sister Katrina's little boy," Kendrick added. "She's married to Matthew Stallion."

"He was sitting with your father and Mr. Briscoe," Vanessa said, trying to connect all the dots.

Kendrick nodded. "Mr. Briscoe is Marah's father and Juanita is her stepmother."

Vanessa nodded.

Marah continued, "The two boys jumping on the trampoline are Michael and Edison. Michael is my sister Marla's son and Edison is my sister Eden's little boy."

"Wow!" Vanessa said, trying to keep the names and faces straight in her head.

Marah laughed. "I'm sure you'll know who's who before the night is out."

"I hope so!"

Marah waved them into the nursery. The room was bright and comfortable with bassinets and rocking chairs. A jungle theme was painted on the wall and just stepping through the door made Vanessa smile.

Kendrick's two sisters-in-law Camryn and Dahlia were inside. Dahlia was nursing one of her infant twins while Camryn cuddled the other against her very pregnant belly. The two women waved excitedly.

Kendrick squinted one eye closed as he leaned to kiss Dahlia's cheek and then Camryn's. "This is Vanessa," he said, pointing in her direction.

"We've heard a lot about you," Dahlia said. "Welcome to the family."

"Thank you!" Vanessa smiled. "I can't believe I'm meeting you," she said, trying to contain her excitement over meeting the famous producer. "I loved your movie *Passionate Premiere*!"

Dahlia laughed. "Thank you."

Marah smiled. "I think that's Cicely on the booby juice and Sidney is in Camryn's arms," she said. "Or vice versa. I can only tell them apart when I'm changing their diapers."

Camryn laughed. "I think Sidney has more hair than his sister. I wish you'd dress them in pink and blue to make it easier for us."

"My babies don't look alike," Dahlia said.

Vanessa smiled. "When are you due?" she asked, pointing at Camryn's very pregnant belly.

"Valentine's Day," she said.

"Wow!" Kendrick said. "That baby is going to be huge!"

Camryn cut her eye at her brother-in-law. "Thank you, Kendrick."

"I'm just saying!"

The women all laughed.

On the way out the door, Vanessa saw Gabrielle and Irene standing in front of a teenaged boy who was playing a game of catch with them. Kendrick gave the young man a wave.

"Hey, Uncle Kendrick!" he called back.

"That's my nephew Collin," Kendrick said, making the introduction. "Collin is my sister Katrina's oldest son."

"Let me show you where you'll be sleeping," Marah said, leading them from the room.

"Is it okay to leave Gabi?" Vanessa asked.

Marah nodded her head. "She'll be fine. Collin is great with the kids, plus he knows he'll earn a little extra allowance babysitting. And there are four nannies. She'll be well taken care of."

It was some ridiculous hour in the morning when the adults found their way to bed. Between last-minute wrapping, the construction of toys and just the merriment of laughing and being together, it had been a long night. Vanessa couldn't remember the last time she'd had so much fun with such a big crowd. But it had been a great time.

There had been games played: Pin the Tail on Santa and Hide the Elf. There'd been a gingerbread house contest, which had paired her and Tarah against Kendrick and John Stallion. Victory for the ladies had bonded the two women. Christmas caroling, eggnog shots and stories of holidays past had made the night memorable. Turning over in the bed Vanessa finally opened her eyes.

"Merry Christmas," Kendrick whispered, rolling his body against hers.

Vanessa turned in his arms. "Merry Christmas! What time is it?"

Kendrick yawned. "Almost seven o'clock."

Shaking herself awake Vanessa lifted herself upright. "Where's Gabi?" she asked, looking to the empty crib against the wall.

Kendrick laughed. "She's been up since daybreak. Irene knocked on the door looking for her and they took off. They're up in the playroom."

Vanessa shook her head. "I didn't even hear them. I'm going to be a horrible mother!"

Kendrick laughed. "I think you'll do just fine."

Vanessa dropped her torso back against the pillows. "I don't know," she said. "I have to be honest, Kendrick, I don't think I'm ready for this. I love Gabrielle to death but I don't think I'm ready for the responsibility."

He took a deep breath. "So what are your options?"

She shrugged. "I'm not sure. As her legal guardian I really have to figure out what's going to be best for her. I really want to finish school and that means going back to New York to finish out the semester. Then I have to think about our relationship. It's just so much!"

Kendrick nodded. "We'll figure it out together, baby. It will all work itself out."

She gave him an easy smile. "Is there anything that makes you crazy? Or are you always so darn calm about everything?"

He laughed. "I'm always calm."

She smiled as Kendrick nuzzled his body against hers, wrapping his arms tightly around her torso. They lay together for some time, warm and comfortable together. A knock on the door pulled them from the quiet.

"Come in!" Kendrick called out.

Maitlyn peeked her head inside. "Merry Christmas!"

"Merry Christmas!" the two chimed in unison.

"The kids are going crazy to open their gifts and breakfast is almost ready," she said. "Y'all need to get up."

Kendrick nodded. "We're on our way. Zak get his gift yet?"

Maitlyn smiled. "Not yet. Did Vanessa get hers?"

Kendrick laughed. "Thank you, Mattie!"

His sister winked an eye before easing back out of the room.

Vanessa jumped up excitedly. "What did Santa bring me?" she asked, her expression childlike.

He shook his head. "You want it now or do you want to open it in front of everyone?"

"That depends. What is it?"

He shook his head. Tossing his legs off the bed he stood up, moving to the closet. He pulled a beautifully wrapped box from his carry-on bag. Moving back to the bed he passed the gift to Vanessa.

Excitement shone on her face as she pulled at the wrapping paper. Inside, there was a silver key ring. The Boudreaux name was engraved on one side. Two keys and a diamond ring were twisted on the band. Vanessa's eyes widened as her gaze flew back and forth between the gift and him.

He pulled the key ring from her hand. Sliding off the diamond he rose from the bed, pulling her to her feet with him. Then he dropped down onto one knee. Lifting his gaze to hers, he gave her a bright smile.

"Vanessa Harrison, will you marry me?" he said.

Her excitement was combustible as she nodded her head yes, throwing her arms around his neck. "Yes! Yes! Yes!" she shouted, clinging to him.

Kendrick kissed her lips, feeling as if everything was right in the world. He pulled her onto his lap as he sat down on the bed. He held out the keys.

"I bought us a home in New Orleans. It's not much, but it's a start. I figure we'll live in New York until you're done with school and then we can go back to Louisiana until we decide what's next for us."

"What about your job?" she asked.

"I have a new job. I was recently hired to handle security for Boudreaux International Hotels and Resorts. It's a suit-and-tie gig with benefits. There's some travel involved but there won't be people shooting at me."

Vanessa threw her arms around his neck a second time and kissed him passionately. "I love you so much!"

The family was on full throttle by the time Vanessa and Kendrick made it downstairs. Delicious smells of food scented the air and laughter was already abundant. Gabrielle sat on John Stallion's lap, watching as Marah cut a waffle into small pieces for her. She sat nicely as she picked the food with her hands, dipping it into a serving of maple syrup Marah had poured on the plate.

"Merry Christmas!" rang throughout the rooms.

"Did you two get any sleep?" John asked, gesturing for the two of them to take a seat.

Kendrick laughed. "Who needs sleep?"

"I hope she hasn't been too much trouble," Vanessa said, gesturing toward Gabi.

John shook his head. "Not at all. Marah and I've been having a good time with her."

Marah nodded in agreement. "She's got an appetite! I've never seen someone so little eat so much!"

Vanessa laughed. "She can eat."

As if on cue Gabi held out a chubby hand gesturing for more. "Bacon, pease!"

John laughed. "She and I are going to be good friends!"

Suddenly an ear-piercing scream rang from across the room. Tarah rushed to where they were standing, pulling at Vanessa's hand. "You got engaged?"

Vanessa laughed, her head bobbing excitedly.

Kendrick shook his head. "Really, Tarah?"

Congratulations rang from one end of the home to the other. Katherine wrapped them both in a warm embrace, tears misting her eyes. Senior gave Vanessa a warm hug, then shook his son's hand.

"Did you speak with her father?" the patriarch questioned.

Kendrick nodded. "Yes, sir. I had a very nice conversation with her father and he gave us his blessing."

The older man nodded. "Good job, son!"

Tarah tossed up her hands. "My God, you people are so old-fashioned!"

Her father dropped an arm around her shoulder. "Call it what you want but any boy wanting to marry you better come see me first if he knows what's good for him."

Kendrick laughed. "I don't think you'll have to worry about that, Senior. Tarah runs them away too fast for any man to even think about marrying her."

His sister shot him a dirty look. "I was happy for you, big brother, but now I think I'm going to tell Vanessa all your dirty secrets. She might change her mind about you once she knows the truth."

There was suddenly another loud shout coming from the adjacent room. Kendrick smiled, recognizing his best friend's deep voice. Zak suddenly came through the door, holding his framed photo above his head.

"It's a boy!" he shouted.

Kendrick laughed, moving to high-five his partner.

Maitlyn moved into the room behind her husband. "Uh, it's a baby. We won't know if it's a boy or girl for a few weeks now."

Standing off to the side Vanessa was overwhelmed by the wealth of happiness that had painted the home with so much love. Kendrick's face was alight with sheer joy. She knew that he had missed times like these with his family and he was quickly trying to make up for lost time.

Looking around the space she found herself grinning widely. This was now her family and she felt completely at home. She turned her attention to Gabi. The little girl was fighting to keep her eyes open as she rested her head against John's chest, her thumb pulled into her mouth. He leaned to kiss the top of her head, brushing her curly locks from her forehead. Marah stood on the other side of the room watching her husband. There was a look of love and longing in her eyes. Vanessa saw her swipe a tear from her eye and imagined that her new friend was feeling as happy as she was. The two women exchanged glances and both smiled.

The morning excitement flew. In the kitchen, dinner preparation had begun and they'd all been shooed out of the space. Kendrick had disappeared someplace with the men and Vanessa was helping the other women clean up the remnants of wrapping paper strewn throughout the family room. The children had all been sent to the nursery, new toys and nap mats in hand. The last time Vanessa had checked Gabi had fallen asleep but she knew it probably wouldn't last for too long.

"You need to relax," Katherine said. "You worry too much. That baby's going to be just fine."

Vanessa nodded. "I know but since her parents died I just want to make sure I do right by her."

Katherine nodded her understanding. "Babies just need a lot of love. Everywhere she goes in this house, that's all she's going to find."

Juanita smiled. "And with all these men around she is definitely safe."

"I just checked on her," Marah said, moving back into the room. "She's still sound asleep."

Vanessa nodded her gratitude.

Kamaya changed the subject. "You two pick a date yet?"

Vanessa shook her head. "Not yet. Everything just happened so fast."

"Well, we can't wait to help you start planning your wedding," the woman said.

"We do great weddings!" Maitlyn exclaimed.

"And baby showers!" Marah added.

"Lord, have mercy!" Katherine exclaimed. She fanned her face with her hands, fighting not to cry.

The women all looked concerned.

"What's wrong, Mama?" Katrina asked, moving to her mother's side.

"I'm just so happy!" the older woman exclaimed. "God is good!"

"All the time!" everyone chimed in reply.

Chapter 17

Kendrick found Vanessa in the small chapel. The space had been adorned with wreaths made of pinecones spray-painted white and tiny red bulbs. The rustic setting was calming, the quiet feeling almost Zen-like. She sat alone on a front pew, deep thought creasing her brow.

He eased into the space and took the seat beside her. "Hey," he said, leaning to kiss her forehead. "Are you okay?"

Vanessa smiled. "I'm happy."

He nodded as he reached for her hand, entwining her fingers with his own. "I missed you. I wanted to make sure you were okay. I know our two families can be overwhelming. It can take some getting used to."

"Actually I've loved every minute with them. Everyone's made me feel so welcome."

"They love you. They know you make me happy."

She took a deep breath, his comment warming her spirit.

Kendrick squeezed her hand. "I want to talk to you about something," he said.

She turned to meet his gaze. "Is something wrong?"

He shook his head. "No. Everything's fine. It's about Gabrielle."

Vanessa felt herself tense.

Kendrick wrapped his arm around her shoulders. "I was thinking about what you said this morning."

"About not being ready to be a mother?"

He nodded.

"I'm being selfish, aren't I?"

"No, you were being honest. And if you don't think you're ready, then I support that. If you told me you wanted to adopt Gabi and a dozen other kids I'd support that, too."

Vanessa suddenly found herself fighting back tears. She took a deep breath. "I know that Gabi is going to need a lot of attention and I keep questioning whether or not it's fair for me to be thinking about school, knowing that's going to take attention away from her. Is it going to be fair of us to move her to New York, then as soon as she gets settled to up and move her again? And is it even fair to put that burden on you and our relationship? I just have so many concerns." She exhaled a heavy sigh.

Kendrick nodded his understanding. "I know you

have concerns, which is why I think I might have a solution."

He spent the next hour sharing his thoughts. And then they prayed. Vanessa found herself smiling, her spirit suddenly feeling rejuvenated. Everything about their decision felt right.

"So, should we run it by them? See what they think?" Kendrick asked.

Vanessa nodded. "I'm so excited," she said. "It would be a little Christmas miracle."

Kendrick smiled his agreement. He pulled his cell phone out of his pocket and called up to the main house. And then they sat waiting.

"This would be a beautiful place to get married," Vanessa said, breaking the silence that had settled around them.

He chuckled softly. "I think so, too." He kissed the side of her face. "But any place you choose will be beautiful."

Minutes later, John, Marah, Katherine and Katrina joined them in the sanctuary.

Marah laughed. "You two want to get married here, don't you?"

Kendrick laughed. "We're thinking about it but that's not why we asked you to join us."

"What's going on, Kendrick?" Katherine asked, dropping onto the pew beside her son.

Kendrick took a deep breath. "Vanessa and I want to talk to John and Marah about something. Katrina, we asked you to join us for your legal advice, and, Mama,

Vanessa and I both respect your opinion. We're hoping you'll give all of us your guidance."

John and Marah slid into the pew behind them. Katrina took a seat on the other side. Everyone was eyeing them both curiously.

Kendrick squeezed Vanessa's hand, urging her on. Vanessa suddenly became emotional and bit down against her bottom lip, fighting not to cry. Marah reached out a hand and squeezed her shoulder. John leaned forward in his seat, concern creasing his forehead.

Vanessa blew out the breath she'd been holding. "You all know that Gabrielle's parents were killed last month. Her grandparents aren't able to take custody of her. Her mother was my best friend and I was asked to assume guardianship if they weren't able to care for her. I love that baby so much and I really want to do what's best for her." Vanessa lifted her eyes to stare at Marah. "Kendrick and I want to know if you two would be willing to adopt her and give her a home."

John and Marah exchanged looks, shock washing over them both.

"But you and Kendrick..." John started.

Kendrick shook his head. "We love Gabi and we want to be in her life but we think, right now, you and Marah would be much better parents than we would be."

"I want to be able to see her grow up," Vanessa added. "I'm a really great Auntie Nessa but I need some time to work up to that mommy title."

John and Marah still stared at each other, a silent conversation being held between their eyes.

Katrina chimed into the conversation. "Legally, with you having guardianship, it would just be a private adoption. I would need to see the parents' will, of course, and then I can draw up the paperwork and file it with the courts for a judge's signature. They'd require a home study but I see no reason why it wouldn't be approved."

Kendrick and Vanessa turned toward his mother. The matriarch had folded her hands in her lap, her eyes closed. Kendrick reached out and gently touched his mother's arm. She opened her eyes slowly, a smile filling her face. Moving onto her feet she kissed her son and then wrapped her arms around Vanessa.

She reached out for Marah's hand and held it. "That baby would be in good hands with you two. She couldn't find a better mommy and daddy to love her."

Marah's tears finally fell past her thick lashes. John wrapped his arms around her and hugged her close. He kissed her mouth, his own tears shining in his eyes.

"Vanessa, I don't know if anyone told you, but Marah and I can't have children," he said, speaking for the first time.

Marah shook her head. "*I* can't have children."

"*We* can't have children," John repeated, the subtle reminder to his wife that they would forever be a team. "I think that both of us had decided that whatever God willed for us, we would accept. But every morning Marah comes out here and asks God to bless us with a child. She didn't think I knew that but I did." He gave his wife a smile before he continued.

"I think I speak for both of us when I tell you Gabi

will want for absolutely nothing. We will love her with everything we have in us." He came to his feet and shook Kendrick's hand. "Thank you."

Marah and Vanessa were both sobbing. Tears turned to laughter as they hugged, jumping up and down with excitement.

Katrina clapped her hands. "I'll get started on the paperwork first thing tomorrow."

Katherine fanned herself, fighting back her own tears. "God is good!"

They made love slowly, a sweet, easy pairing that touched both their souls. As Vanessa lay beneath him she was consumed with pleasure and clung to him, needing to feel him against her. She moved with him, matching him stroke for stroke, and they both felt themselves slipping toward the highs of ecstasy. She was suddenly lost in the spasms of bliss.

They clung to each other as they reveled in the sweetest sensations. When her breathing had calmed and his heartbeat returned to normal, he planted a gentle kiss against the back of her neck.

"Why are you crying, baby?" Kendrick asked softly. He brushed a tear from her cheek.

She thought back to their first Christmas together. She and Kendrick had pledged their commitment to each other and she anticipated being his wife before the new year. Gabrielle had fallen asleep in Marah's arms and she and John had slipped right into their new roles with ease. The support of the Boudreaux and Stallion families had been abundant and as Kendrick's mother had reminded them all, family was nothing without love.

Kendrick lifted himself up on his elbow. He rolled her gently, staring down at her. Love was like gold in his eyes. "What is it, baby?"

Vanessa smiled. "This has been the best holiday I've ever had."

* * * * *

REQUEST YOUR FREE BOOKS!

2 FREE NOVELS PLUS 2 FREE GIFTS!

KIMANI™ ROMANCE

Love's ultimate destination!

YES! Please send me 2 FREE Harlequin® Kimani™ Romance novels and my 2 FREE gifts (gifts are worth about $10). After receiving them, if I don't wish to receive any more books, I can return the shipping statement marked "cancel." If I don't cancel, I will receive 4 brand-new novels every month and be billed just $5.19 per book in the U.S. or $5.74 per book in Canada. That's a savings of at least 20% off the cover price. It's quite a bargain! Shipping and handling is just 50¢ per book in the U.S. and 75¢ per book in Canada.* I understand that accepting the 2 free books and gifts places me under no obligation to buy anything. I can always return a shipment and cancel at any time. Even if I never buy another book, the two free books and gifts are mine to keep forever.

168/368 XDN F4XC

Name	(PLEASE PRINT)	
Address		Apt. #
City	State/Prov.	Zip/Postal Code

Signature (if under 18, a parent or guardian must sign)

Mail to the Harlequin® Reader Service:
IN U.S.A.: P.O. Box 1867, Buffalo, NY 14240-1867
IN CANADA: P.O. Box 609, Fort Erie, Ontario L2A 5X3

Want to try two free books from another line?
Call 1-800-873-8635 or visit www.ReaderService.com.

* Terms and prices subject to change without notice. Prices do not include applicable taxes. Sales tax applicable in N.Y. Canadian residents will be charged applicable taxes. Offer not valid in Quebec. This offer is limited to one order per household. Not valid for current subscribers to Harlequin® Kimani™ Romance books. All orders subject to credit approval. Credit or debit balances in a customer's account(s) may be offset by any other outstanding balance owed by or to the customer. Please allow 4 to 6 weeks for delivery. Offer available while quantities last.

Your Privacy—The Harlequin® Reader Service is committed to protecting your privacy. Our Privacy Policy is available online at www.ReaderService.com or upon request from the Harlequin Reader Service.

We make a portion of our mailing list available to reputable third parties that offer products we believe may interest you. If you prefer that we not exchange your name with third parties, or if you wish to clarify or modify your communication preferences, please visit us at www.ReaderService.com/consumerschoice or write to us at Harlequin Reader Service Preference Service, P.O. Box 9062, Buffalo, NY 14269. Include your complete name and address.

KROM13R

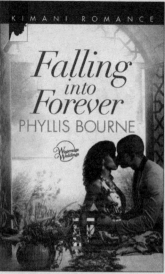

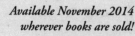

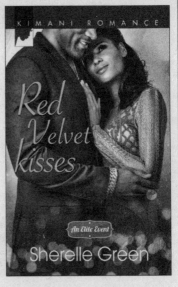